The Angel

ROBERT M WHITBEY

Small Town Hero Series Book #1

DEDICATION

Dedicated to my family, who have always been a source of love and support.

Preface

The traditional Superhero story usually takes place in a large city. These cities often become a character in the story. Think about it. What would Batman be without Gotham city, or Spiderman without New York? Growing up in California's great Central Valley, I always wondered how heroes like Spiderman or Batman would fare in an area with no skyscrapers.

This is largely why I wrote The Angel. The story takes place in Kern County, CA, where I grew up wanting to be Spiderman and Batman. We explore what life would be like to have super powers, but live in an area where everyone knows you. How hard would it be to hide it? What types of sacrifices would your family and you have to make to keep you safe?

This is the first of what I hope will become a series of books dealing with the same topic: Small Town Heroes. The type of heroes you might find in flyover country and who wish to stay in flyover country. The sad reality is if real super powers existed, there are just too many people that would want access to them. The powerful may want nothing more than to work a job and come home at night to a family that loves them. The powerless would likely hate them for it and want to use them in some way.

I hope you enjoy reading The Angel. If you are from Kern County, you're going to be familiar with a lot of the locations. If you're not from Kern County, consider visiting. It's a lovely place filled with lovely people. Except during Summer. Stay away during Summer.

- Rob

Chapter 1

Tom Salem's divorce was final and he is currently standing on the edge of a cliff, staring at the river through the trees hundreds of feet below. The water level is low and the rocks are high. No way that would he survive the fall, and that was his plan. Without Tanya, without the other one, he had no reason to keep pretending he wanted to live.

It was a crisp, moonlit summer night in the Sierra's. He had driven for over an hour to find this spot, this last little perfect view to be his last. He loved these mountains and had stood at this spot countless times in his 30 years, just soaking in the view. He took his shoes off and put everything from his pockets in them. He had written a note but decided against leaving it for someone to find. It would be obvious what happened since the shoes were there. And anyone that knew him would know why he did it. They might find the body, but probably not. His point of entry into the Tule River would be too remote and the impact would likely leave his body in pieces anyway.

He took several deep breaths. The thick pine scent almost made him feel drunk. He began to hum a song silently. *He stopped loving her today*...he closed his eyes, took one long step, and began to fall.

Time seemed to slow. Tom wasn't expecting to have so much time to analyze his decision. His heart drummed in his chest as he realized how his actions would affect those he left behind. Like all those that have took this route before, he was suddenly filled with regret. Bracing himself for the impact, he kept his eyes shut tight. He was, after all, a coward.

The impact finally came but from a different direction than expected. Something hit his side very hard, knocking the wind out of him and changing his trajectory sideways. It felt like he was shot with a cannon. He felt himself hit the cliff-side, but it was soft. *Cliffs aren't soft,* he thought. He tried to open his eyes but the pain in his side made him wince tightly and his mind began to fade. As he drifted off, he heard a voice saying to him, "stay with me, buddy!" But he couldn't fight the pull towards unconsciousness.

He awoke in his car. The pain in his right side prominent as he straightened up, letting him know he hadn't dreamed it. He remembered jumping off the cliff. He remembered falling. But then what? One moment he plummeted to his death, the next in his car. *How on earth am I in my car?* He thought.

Tom glanced at the clock on the dashboard. It was just passed midnight. Two hours had passed since he stepped out on the edge of that cliff. Two hours he had been out. And, somehow, he was back in his car. He turned to look around the area and immediately regretted it. The shooting pain radiating in all directions from his right side made him cry out. He had broken ribs before, but this was worse. He almost blacked out again.

Then he noticed lights coming up the hill. Not just headlights, but flashing lights. *An ambulance?* It pulled up to his driver side and two EMT's got out looking around as if they were not sure what to expect. Both were male, one tall, one a little shorter.

The shorter EMT knocked on his window. Tom thought about rolling it down, but remembered the pain associated with movement.

"Did you call for an ambulance?" the man asked with a slightly raised voice through the glass.

Tom didn't know how to react. *Had I called?* He was confused.

Again, he asked, "Sir, are you okay? Did you call for an ambulance?" This time he raised his voice almost to a yell.

10

Tom slowly shook his head no. His brain was foggy. *Did I hit my head?* He remembered the drive up. He remembered being determined to jump from that cliff. He remembered closing his eyes and stepping off. After that he remembered the pain in his side and then waking up in his car.

The other EMT said, "hey, there are shoes over there by the edge. Are they his?"

"I don't know, he's hurt or stoned or something," he answered. "Sir, are you hurt? Do you need help?"

Tom slowly shook his head in the affirmative.

"Sir, my name is Steve. I'm an EMT. You look like you're hurting pretty bad and we need to check you out. We can't do it from out here. I'm going to open the door slowly."

Tom continued to nod okay and his body began to tense up from the pain he knew he was about to feel when they moved him.

As Steve opened the door, he asked, "what's your name, sir?"

"Tom. Tom Salem," he spat through clenched teeth. The driver side door opened completely and the other EMT, his name tag read Dave, assisted his partner. He had come around the passenger side and opened the door to get a better look.

"What happened to you, sir?" Dave asked as he examined Tom for damage.

"I think I slipped off the edge and caught myself before I fell all the way off. I must have banged my side pretty hard because my ribs are screaming right now."

"Wow," Dave remarked. "You are one lucky dude."

The EMT's managed to get Tom out of the vehicle and into the ambulance. They got him settled on a gurney and started an IV. They couldn't give him much for pain, so he had a long ride to Porterville ahead of him.

As Steve took down Tom's information, Dave took one last look around the area. He grabbed Tom's shoes before climbing into the driver's seat.

Steve leaned into the front and indicated they were ready to roll. Dave moved closer to Steve , "Ya know, no one takes their shoes off unless they're gonna jump." Steve just shrugged in reply.

Chapter 2

Porterville Evangelical Hospital was not huge, but it did have a state of the art emergency room. Tom felt much better thanks to the pain medicine and the warm bed-side manner of the staff. He had three broken ribs that hurt like the dickens when he tried to raise his right arm, even with the meds. Still, he felt a lot better than he did during his long ride down the mountain.

With the pain no longer dizzying his brain, his thoughts turned to his failed suicide attempt. He knew he had stepped off that edge. He could remember the feeling of falling and the sudden change of direction. He remembered *the voice* telling him he 'had him.' He didn't hit the ground, he knew that for sure.

It was possible he hit a tree branch on the way down, but he hadn't seen any that close to the cliff-side. *Had he hit a ledge and tumbled?* Maybe, but how did he get back in his car? And who called the ambulance? And who spoke to him before he passed out?

Maybe the meds were making me fuzzy, he thought. None of this made any sense to him. In the morning, he would be discharged. Then he could get to the bottom of things. For now, sleep beckoned.

In the morning, he called his dad, Bill for a ride. He hadn't called him the night before because he didn't want to worry him. His lie wasn't the best, but it worked. His divorce finalized, he had gone up the mountain to toss his wedding ring off a cliff. As he threw it, he slipped and fell, hitting his side on a large rock. He "admitted" to having a few drinks first to make it a little more believable.

An hour later, he and his dad were on the way up the mountain to pick up his car. They didn't speak much except for idle chit-chat. The lie seemed to work just fine, but not completely. A parent knows when their child is not telling the whole truth, but Tom's dad was never one to pry. He knew there was more to the story which would come out in due time.

As they approached the small turn-out, Tom spotted his car right where he left it. It was dustier now, likely because of the ambulance throwing up a lot of dirt when they sped off. They both got out and Tom fished his keys out of his plastic hospital bag. He opened the car and got in to start it up. The pain associated with his movement reminded him he needed another pain pill soon.

"Where is the rock you hit?" Bill asked.

"I'm not sure, it was dark and I was a little light headed," Tom said.

"I guess it's lucky you didn't have an accident on the way up," Bill postulated.

Tom noted a lack of empathy in his voice. It was clear Bill wasn't fully buying the story.

"Sure is a long drop," Bill noticed. "A person falls off here, they'd probably never find them."

"That's why I was going to throw my ring off it," Tom replied.

"You still wanna do it?" Bill asked. "Throw your ring, I mean?"

Tom paused. "Considering what happened, I think the universe is telling me not to. Maybe I'll do it later."

"Well, next time, give me a call first and I'll come with you. Designated driver and all that," Bill said.

Tom started his car and let it warm up for a minute. His dad, satisfied that the car was in good shape, asked Tom if he would be okay to drive with 'that bum right side.'

"I'll be okay. I'll just take it slow. Give the brakes a work out." After a few more minutes of chit chat, Tom's dad began his drive down the mountain with Tom assuring him he was right behind him.

After waiting a few more minutes and not knowing why, Tom put the car in drive and pulled out on the road. Like he promised, he drove slowly through the hairpin turns. About a mile down the twisty mountain road, he noticed an old, blue Ford truck parked in another pullout. It was not uncommon to see trucks along the road as people often pulled off and hiked down to the river to fish. It was usually just a short jaunt down a rocky hillside to the river. Most of the gravel pullouts were not high cliffs like where he had been the night before.

The pullout was just barely bigger than the truck and located on a curve on the uphill side of the road. Tom had to slow to a crawl to make the sharp turn in case someone was coming in the other direction. He thought for a second. *Was that truck there last night?* He thought for a moment and replayed the drive in his mind. He had slowed and swerved to miss that same truck. Yet, he didn't remember the ambulance slowing down or swerving at that turn. Odd that they would have left, but come back the next day.

Tom continued his drive down the mountain. He would start to let his mind drift a bit but he really needed to concentrate on the drive due to its constant hairpin turns. His mind would drift to Tanya and her constant look of disappointment, then trudge to other, less savory images and he would snap back to his driving.

An hour and a half later, he pulled into his apartment complex in Bakersfield. He hadn't expected to be back. His apartment was sparse even though he had been there for over a year. It was cheap and that was what he needed when he was forced out of his home. A studio apartment in a middle-class area with only a small number of welfare queens and drug dealers interspersed with the entry level professionals, oilfield workers, and retirees.

He had cleaned it up before he left and boxed what few belongings he had brought to the apartment. He had even written people's names on the boxes so no one would have to sort through them. Dad's name was on the box with all his childhood mementos. Tanya's name was on all the boxes with paperwork and their shared mementos. A few friends with their own boxes for things they would like. And then he saw the box with the other one's name on it. Of course, she would have never gotten it, but it seemed fitting to put her stuff in there.

It was early in the afternoon and he hadn't eaten so he made a peanut butter and jelly sandwich. A little depression in the peanut butter filled with extra jelly, just like the other one liked it. It tasted so good. He followed it up with a glass of milk to wash it down. He ate over the sink, which was fairly common for him since moving to his 'bachelor pad'.

He sat in his one piece of furniture, a recliner. He removed his dad's name tag from it. He stretched out and lay back, staring at the ceiling. His ribs were aching and he thought about getting a pain pill, but didn't move. He thought about his ex-wife and the other one. He thought about his decision to commit suicide. He wondered if he still felt the desire to do it. He didn't, he decided. Signing the final divorce papers had carried him down a very sad path that ultimately led to the edge of a cliff. He was convinced there was a reason he was alive, and he desperately wanted to know why.

The next day, Tom went to work. He had worked for The Bakersfieldian, a local newspaper, for nearly 8 years. He was technically a columnist, not a reporter, and while paper circulation had dwindled, he had a good-sized online audience. He hadn't expected to see the place again, but hadn't taken the time to clean out his office like he did his apartment. There wasn't much there anyway–a coffee mug, a picture of Tanya and the other one in his top drawer, his personal laptop. The furniture all belonged to the office, not him.

Today he had a new story to write. This was the story of a suicidal man given a second chance. It would be written from the perspective of a guy telling him his story in a bar. A few people that were familiar with him would probably figure out it was about him, but that didn't matter. This was therapy and he wasn't that guy anymore. He felt a purpose, though he didn't know what it was.

Two hours later, the story was written and submitted to his editor, Sam Winston. He celebrated the same way he always celebrated after writing a good article, by getting a cup of coffee. *Jenkies!* had been a fixture in downtown Bakersfield for over 30 years. The current owner, everyone called her Velma but her name was actually Peggy, greeted him at the door. She had inherited the shop from her father Shaggy (actually Ben) when he retired 3 years ago.

"Finished another article, Mr. Salem?" She asked.

"I've asked you to call me Tom for years, Velma," he replied.

"What, are we dating now?" she smirked.

"No, but Mr. Salem is my dad. Creeps me out a bit." Tom laughed.

"I know. That's why it's so fun. So, you want the usual?"

"Sure," Tom replied. She brought him his large black coffee and he sipped on it for a few minutes before checking his messages on his phone. Not surprised, he already saw a message from Sam.

Are You serious? Sam wrote.

Yes, he replied.

A few minutes later, Sam replied, *I think we need to talk about the ramifications before we print it.*

Tom replied, *I understand the ramifications. Please print it as I wrote it. Also, I'm taking a week off if that's alright.*

Sam replied, *MORE than alright. I insist. Take however long you need, but keep me apprised.*

Tom put his phone away and sipped his coffee. Tomorrow will likely be a long day.

Chapter 3

The next day was indeed a long day. Tom's article went out with the morning edition (the afternoon edition was online only). By 9am, his cell phone and email were blowing up. Most were from long time readers, but also other media outlets and some friends and family. He ignored them all except the unavoidable call from his dad. That was along conversation, but it ended on good terms, his dad assured that his attempt would not be repeated.

His plan for everyone else was to play dumb. Don't confirm or deny anything. That way, the story would still have an air of mystery. Was it him who jumped or did he indeed get this story second hand? All through his breakfast, his phone continued to buzz and he continued to ignore it. Emails, text messages, phone calls, even comments on the article's website would all cause the phone to buzz. And he kept ignoring them.

After finishing his cereal over the kitchen sink, he passed by his phone when it buzzed. He absently glanced down and saw the person calling. It was Tanya. He knew she would call eventually, but he didn't want to talk to her. In fact, if he knew her as well as he thought, she was probably calling as she was driving over. He really wished he hadn't given her his address to forward his mail.

He quickly dressed, aggravating his ribs, and got to his car. He didn't want to talk to her right now. He pulled out of his parking lot and realized he had no idea where he was headed. *Jenkies!* sounded good, but too many people from work would be there. He kept driving until he saw a small coffee shop and pulled in.

Tom went inside and ordered a cup of black coffee. There were only a few people scattered around inside, and a few others had wandered in as he took a seat in the corner and pulled out his laptop. *Time to start answering emails*, he thought. Most of the emails were complimentary, calling him a 'hero' for 'coming clean about his struggle.' He came up with a thankful reply, then cut and pasted it to about a dozen emails. *Ridiculous*, he thought. *That I would be considered a hero. I tried to take the easy way out, but was stopped. If I had succeeded would I still be called a hero? No, this was a confession of failure. Failure to do something as simple as take a long walk off a short path and now I have to deal with why I'm still alive. Certainly, a hero would have never been at the top of that cliff to begin with!*

He continued to paste his reply when he came across a different email. This was from a reader he knew well. Pete Zisk, no idea if it was his real name, operated a website dealing with unexplained phenomenon in Kern County. Haunted houses, ghostly figures along back roads, and UFO sightings were covered in great length at KernCountySupernatural.com. He usually heard from Zisk a lot during the month of October when he wrote stories relating to Halloween and a few other times throughout the year.

The subject line read, "PLEASE CONTACT ME!!!" Seemed like an odd request. Tom didn't think he was a therapist or councilor or anything like that. He assumed he was jobless and lived in his mom's basement. He opened the email and it read:

There may be more to this, Tom. You are not the first person something like this has happened to. I need to meet with you if you are willing. I think I can help you find some answers.

PZ

PS: Please don't write it off as a miracle or some such non-sense.

PSS: Glad you didn't die.

Tom's immediate reaction was to laugh. It was his rule to never meet with readers outside of work activities that required it. Some of these people were nuts, and Zisk seemed nuttier than most. But as he rescanned the email, one line popped out at him. *You are not the first person something like this has happened to.* Tom had a lot of questions about what had happened to him. Could Zisk provide those answers? He decided to chance it and typed a reply.

Where should I meet you? Tom typed.

It didn't take long for an answer. *I'm already here.*

Tom looked around as a tall, overweight man with longish brown hair, an unkempt beard and thick glasses got up and approached him. Tom had seen him come in not long after he did, but thought he was a transient. As he got to the table, he stuck out his hand.

"Hi Tom, I'm Pete Zisk."

Tom shook his hand. "Nice to meet you, Pete," he said warily. "Did you follow me here?"

"Yeah, I know it sounds creepy, but it would have been creepier if I'd shown up at your door." He took a seat across from Tom.

"How did you know where I live," Tom asked.

"There are no secrets on the internet, Tom. Can I call you Tom?"

"Uh, sure," he replied. Tom was obviously taken aback by Pete's forwardness, but was willing to listen to him.

"Great, you can call me Pete. Or PZ. Doesn't matter. What does matter is your story."

21

"Right, Pete, you said you might have some answers…"

"First, some background info. You wrote that you closed your eyes, stepped off the cliff, and was hit by something and blacked out. When you woke up, you were in your car and an ambulance was on its way. Is that about right?"

"In a nutshell, yeah, but I never said it was me…"

"Come on, Tom, after what you've been through the last 2 years, no one would have been surprised if they found you dead. So let's drop the pretense, okay?"

Tom nodded his head in the affirmative.

"As you know, my website catalogs all the strange occurrences, past and present, in Kern County. There is a wealth of odd history in this area and KernCountySupernatural.com catalogs it all."

"I've seen the website, Pete," Tom interrupted. "What specifically do you want me to know?"

"Okay, to the point, very good. I tend to drift, so let me know if I'm doing that too much." He took out a large tablet PC and flipped it around for Tom to see. There was a picture of an older man with a cane, obviously favoring one leg over the other. "I have several interesting oddities that have happened in the last 10 years. This one involves a man named Duggan. About 5 years ago he was cutting firewood, illegally I might add, about 12 miles from Springville. He misjudged the fall angle and the tree landed on his leg, pinning him underneath. After a few minutes of struggling, he passed out. He woke up being loaded into an ambulance. He lost the leg, but he's still alive."

"So how is that like my story, other than the woods," Tom asked.

"Duggan was alone and over a mile from his truck. He had ridden an ATV to the cut site. Nobody lived nearby; no hiking trails exist in that area. His cell phone was shattered by the tree. He woke up a mile away from where he was pinned by that tree. The ATV was still at the cut site. The EMT's said they received a call but no name was left. They assumed it was someone who had been with him that didn't want to get in trouble for cutting trees illegally."

"That sounds like a reasonable explanation," Tom observed.

"I spoke with Duggan. He had no reason to lie to me, I'm not a cop. Frankly, he is still shook by it. Started going to church. Stopped drinking. According to him, losing his leg is the best thing that ever happened to him."

Tom was skeptical, and it must have shown on his face. He had heard stories like this before, but not being a religious man himself, he usually chalked it up to hysteria of some sort.

Zisk changed the picture on the screen one showing a teenage girl. "This girl is named Ellie. A couple of years ago she was hiking with her family not far from Balch Park, which is about 15 miles from Duggan's tree. She got separated briefly when she left the trail to go to the bathroom. She slid down a ravine and hit her head. As her family searched, she stumbled around trying to find her way. She lost her glasses at some point and became hopelessly lost."

"I remember this," Tom remembered. "People from all over Kern and Tulare counties were looking for her. They even had helicopters. Didn't they find her someplace weird?"

"Yeah, after being gone for 5 days, they found her delirious and sitting in a lawn chair next to the Fire Department in Springville. She even had a half empty water bottle sitting next to her on the ground.

That was almost 20 miles from where she went missing, over the worst terrain you could ever imagine."

Tom had a faraway look, showing he was thinking. "Still, she could have wandered there in 5 days. Not exactly unheard of."

"Except she was half-blind without her glasses. She says she wandered along a dry creek. She stated she moved uphill because she thought there might be people fishing upstream where there was water. After a few days, she passed out from lack of food and proper hydration. According to her, she woke up in the arms of a 'giant Cyclops.' He gave her water and 'flew' her down the mountain to the fire department."

"You interviewed her, too?"

"Yep, with her parents, of course. She's only 15 and I'm a big, weird-looking guy with an internet site. She still maintains she was rescued by a giant 'Cyclops.' She said he smelled like cotton. Her dad is a cotton farmer in Porterville so she knows the smell well."

"So what are you saying, Mr. Zisk? There's a flying Cyclops helping people in the woods?" Tom started to say the words in all seriousness, but by the time they came out, it sounded condescending.

"It's not just the woods, Tom. I have records of people being saved all over northern Kern County, sometimes under the most incredible circumstances. Some attribute their safety to a mystical person, others can't explain it." He flipped to another photo. This one was of an elderly Hispanic woman. "This is Maria. Maria was closing up her small, Mexican food market in downtown Shafter one night when two guys jumped her and stole her purse. They ran down an alley. As Maria got up off the ground, her purse flew back out of the alley and she heard a man scream. She called the police and they found both guys unconscious with, get this, all four of their arms broken severely. Cops said they were drunk and got into a fight over the purse. The men say they were jumped by 4 other guys, but there was no evidence of it."

He flipped to another picture. This one showed a burned-out building. "This is the former residence of Homer Todd. He lived out in the country between Shafter and Wasco. Homer was 80 and had mobility issues. He could walk, but pretty slow going. One night, two years ago, he goes to bed and later wakes up, still in his bed, sitting in his front yard with his house ablaze. His neighbor was there. He had seen the fire from his house and when he got there, he found Homer out on his lawn, still asleep in his bed."

"Sounds farfetched," Tom said.

"You want farfetched? His bedroom was on the second floor. Though there was no reported explosion, pieces of his bedroom wall were found 100 yards from the house."

Tom thought for a second. "So, he and his bed were possibly blown out of the room through the wall on the second floor..." Tom stopped. He had to admit, that sounded absolutely ridiculous. "So, how do you explain these things?"

Pete Zisk smiled. "Believe it or not, Tom, I don't like to speculate. I never publish pure speculation on my website. I only offer 'possibilities' and even then, I need something of substance to back it up."

"Why do I think you have a 'possibility' to offer in this case?" Tom asked.

Pete smiled and looked down at the table. He then shook his head a little as if he was having an inner dialogue. "Kern County has a guardian angel, Tom. Not the kind that swoops down out of the sky, doing the will of God and all that, but someone or something is helping people out when they need it most. And whoever they are, they don't want any publicity."

Tom finished his coffee in one gulp and stood up, gathering his things. "Mr. Zisk," he said. "Thank you for your time, but this is all a bit much to take in. I don't know if any of this has anything to do with what happened to me, but it's all very interesting. I'm gonna leave now and I would rather you not follow me this time."

"Just think about it, Tom. Take my card. The more you investigate, the more you will see there are no coincidences. Just cause and effect."

Tom smiled and picked up the card, then walked out the door. As he got into his car, he looked around and saw the only other car was an old, dusty El Camino. He quickly pulled out of the parking lot, checking to see if he was being followed. No other cars pulled out.

He needed to go somewhere and think. He needed to answer emails. He didn't want to see anyone face to face for a while. It would be better to let things blow over. But where could he go?

Then it came to him. There was a perfect place for him to go to get away from it all. He turned his car onto Hwy 99 and headed towards Springville.

Chapter 4

Tuolumne Springs Bed and Breakfast was a small, off the beaten path place with 5 large bedrooms. Just a few miles outside of Springville, it was a romantic getaway for many couples looking to literally get away from it all. Not many people knew about it and that is how the owner, Tilly, liked it. She met Tom at the door.

"Mr. Salem, so good to see you," she greeted.

"Hi Tilly. Got any rooms?" Tom asked.

"Got 5 empty rooms right now. How long you lookin' to stay?"

"Let's start with two days," Tom said.

"No problem. You want your…regular…?" Tilly asked.

"No, I'll take the small one on the main floor if I can."

"Alright. You hungry? I can make you a sandwich if you like."

"Nah, I ate on the way here. I'm just gonna stow my stuff, then head up the mountain for a few hours."

"Well, you know the drill. Doors lock at 11pm. Dinner is on your own, but since you're the only one here, you know where the fridge is. I'll have breakfast ready at 7am if I don't see you tonight. Just yell if you need anything."

"Thanks, Tilly." Tom went to his room and stored his stuff. He only brought a couple of changes of clothes and some assorted sundries he picked up on the way up. He didn't want to go back to his apartment in case Tanya was waiting. He grabbed a flashlight, water bottle, and his phone to take with him, and went back to his car.

As he headed back up the mountain, he thought about where he headed. He wanted to see the cliff he had jumped from. Not at the top, but from the bottom. Maybe he'd find a clue as to what had happened to him at the bottom. It meant a short hike to get there.

He reached the cliff 30 minutes later. He decided he would backtrack down the mountain to see where he could hike in to its foot. He took an old shirt out of his car he used as a rag and threw it down to the bottom of the cliff. That would make it easy to tell when he found the foot of the cliff. Things would look very different from down there. He didn't see it hit bottom, but he did see it disappear between the craggy cliff-side and the tree canopy.

He drove slowly back down the road and came to the small pullout where the blue truck had been. He pulled off on to it and, sure enough, looking down he could see the river. It was an easy climb down, 50 feet or so with a good slant. Even with his ribs still hurting, he should be able to do it.

As he edged down, he couldn't help but notice how beautiful the area was with thick trees, big granite boulders dotting the mountainside, and the fast-moving water snaking through the large canyon. If not for the occasional car passing by on the road above, it seemed almost like another world.

He reached the bottom, and was about 10 feet from the river. There he saw another unfortunate sign of human activity. Trash. Though not a lot, he saw beer bottle caps, cigarette stubs and the odd fishing tackle. There was also a trash can with a little trash in it. It had a heavy lid to keep the small critters out, but it wouldn't stop a bear.

He looked up the north side of the river, back towards the cliff bottom he had intended to be his final resting place. He walked in that direction for about half a mile until the canyon narrowed. It had been rather easy up to that point, walking on large boulders and hard packed ground. However, at the narrowing, there were several downed trees blocking the path. He could probably climb them with some difficulty. He pulled out his phone and began to snap pictures all around him. Where he had climbed down, where he had walked in, the trees blocking the path, the opposite side of the river, and anything else he could see. He didn't know why he took the pictures, but it seemed like the thing to do.

He studied the trees blocking the path and plotted the easiest way over. The opposite side of the river was not blocked, but it was about 70 feet across from this point and the water was moving swiftly. Though not deep, it would be very cold and he could be swept away. No reason to chance it. So he began to climb over, favoring his unhurt side. It took him a few minutes to reach the top but he finally made it and started down the much easier back side.

The forest was very thick on this side of the fallen trees. You could not see the road at top and Tom couldn't hear any cars pass by. The thick foliage made it darker, too. Not like night, but certainly shady. There was a clear path tromped down along the river and he followed it.

After what seemed like a mile or so, he saw the shirt he had tossed down in a tree above him. He stepped a little closer to the cliff-side and looked up. He saw the cliff's edge clearly from this angle. It was funny to him that he couldn't see the ground from the top, but could see the top from the ground. All the foliage and rocks played tricks on your perception.

Just then, the enormity of the situation hit him like a brick. Where he was standing was full of large, jagged rocks. The ground was ugly and stark, while the view, with all the trees and the river flowing by was beautiful. This is where his body would have lain for a while anyway. It wasn't as remote as he thought as he had hiked it relatively easily. His body wouldn't have landed in the river at all. But he would definitely have died from the impact.

Feeling his knees weaken, he sat down on a large, dusty boulder. His mind began to wander to Tanya and the other one. He actually began to feel the despair setting in again when he noticed footprints. They were all over the boulders. Large boots from the look of it, much larger than his foot, yet not gigantic, maybe a size 13. Somebody had been down here recently.

He began to study the ground more closely. Unlike the area he first climbed down to, there was not a single scrap of trash around. Odd considering someone had certainly spent a lot of time right here. Whoever it was obviously respected this land a lot. *Most likely a hippy with big feet,* Tom thought.

Lots of activity in this area, though, he thought. *Could there have been someone down here that night?* He looked around more, trying to see if the footprints told a story like the trackers in a movie. Unfortunately, he was no tracker. Just a bunch of big footprints. He stepped back a little to see the ground better. As he stepped again, he fell backwards into the swiftly flowing Tule River.

It was really cold and moving very fast, but it was only three feet deep in this stretch. Still, each time he tried to stand up he fell back down and slid further down the river. Slowly but surely, he made his way towards the bank. He floated and splashed his way past where he had originally come down the hillside, and pulled himself out of the river. He was soaked and freezing. More than one curse word emanated from his lips. Luckily, he had managed to keep hold of his phone.

He sat on the bank and leaned back all the way, looking up. He thought about how much his ribs ached from the cold and the exertion.

The tree canopy was too thick to see the blue sky, but something caught his eye on the trunk of the tree next to him. He stood up and saw it was exactly what he thought it was: a game camera. Someone obviously hunted this area and sat up this game camera to see if there were any four legged visitors. Its lens was pointed right at the trail he was just on. If someone or something had been on that trail a few nights ago, it may have got a picture.

He examined it closely. He wasn't a hunter, but he had used these cameras before in college to study wildlife in a class he took. They were simple to operate and although this one could be locked up, it did not have a padlock on it. He unbuckled it from the tree and popped the camera open. He slid out the SD card, then closed it and remounted it to the tree. It was a cardinal sin among hunters to do such a thing, but he hoped the hunter would forgive the minor larceny. He would have swapped his phones SD card for it, but it was completely soaked.

He made his way up the side of the hill and reached his car. He took a towel out of the back and put it in his seat, then sat down, started it up and drove back down the mountain. In a little while, he was back at the B&B. He took a quick, warm shower and found a candy bar in the bag of sundries he bought on the way up.

He slid the SD card in the card reader on his laptop and transferred all the photos over. It would make scanning the photos faster, since there were hundreds. Apparently, the camera had been there for a while. Luckily, they had a time and date stamp on each one. He jumped through them until he reached the day he was looking for. The night pictures were clear, but all in black and white. He looked through the dozen or so pictures from the appointed time frame.

One by one he stared at the pictures, triggered by the local wildlife and some blurry blobs. Then he spotted what he was looking for: the image of a large man at the very edge of what the camera could

31

adequately pick up. It was slightly out of focus, but he appeared to be wearing a ball cap with a large "C" surrounding a little "A" written on the front. Obviously a UC, Davis Aggies fan. He wore a plaid, short-sleeved button-up shirt and blue jeans. He looked like 90% of the young farmers in the area. No camo, though, and no rifle, so he wasn't likely a hunter. Unfortunately, it was just too blurry to make out the face.

In the first picture, the *man in plaid* was coming from the area of the fallen trees. According to the time stamp, it was about midnight. Of course, that could be wrong if the hunter hadn't programmed it right. Tom would have been just waking up in his car about that time. Had the *man in plaid* seen what happened? Had he called the ambulance? Or was Pete right and this was the 'Angel?' He re-examined the images with the burry blobs. Those blurs looked an awful lot liked stretched plaid. "How fast would he have to be moving to leave a blurry image?" Tom wondered aloud.

Tom wondered if Pete would have some sort of software that could enhance the picture. Heck, Pete probably had software that could go through all these pictures and find a better image, too. But Pete was not a journalist. He was an 'information whore' as his colleagues put it. He was in the business of disseminating information to the people, whether it was true or false, researched or just a tip from an anonymous source. The *man in plaid* could just be a hiker or hunter and Tom didn't want Pete plastering his photo all over the internet. No, Pete would be left out for the time being.

Chapter 5

The next morning, Tom used Tilly's printer to print out the best picture he had of the *man in plaid*. For a B&B with such rustic charm, Tilly prided herself on having good technology for her guests. After eating a large breakfast with Tilly, and some polite conversation, Tom went back to his room to get ready for the day. Tilly, who always ate with her guests, had offered to wash his clothes from the day prior and Tom had happily accepted.

The night before, he had placed his wet phone in a jar of dry rice to try and dry it out. He had seen the trick on the web somewhere. He decided to leave it there today and instead borrowed a small digital camera from Tilly in case he needed to document something. His small bag packed for the day, he grabbed the photo and headed for his car.

Tom was going to spend the day showing the picture to some of the various businesses in the area. There were a few restaurants, bars, souvenir shops, bait shops and tiny grocery stores up the mountain. It may be that someone knows the man in plaid if he lives in the area or at least frequents it.

He spent the entire morning going to shops in and around Springville with no luck. Most of the shop owners were elderly and their memories weren't great. Some spoke scattered English. Others just flat out refused to talk to him much because he wasn't a local. Mountain folk can be that way at times, even when they rely on the out-of-towners for their living.

After grabbing a bite, Tom decided to head up the mountain to some of the smaller towns. There were small stores scattered around here and there. He found some closed without explanation; others were open for only a few hours a day during the week. Those that were open looked at the picture, but didn't know him. One guy said he looked very familiar but "couldn't put his finger on it." By dinner time, Tom was on his way back to Tilly's disheartened.

As he came in the door, Tilly called to him that she was just finishing dinner if he was interested. Tom replied, "Sure," and sat his stuff by the door. He folded the picture up and put it in his breast pocket. He washed his hands at the kitchen sink, and he and Tilly sat down to eat.

"You look beaten down," Tilly remarked.

"You always tell it like it is, don't you Tilly?" Tom replied.

"You never did tell me what you were up to today," she prodded.

Tom shook his weary head. "I spent the day showing this stupid blurry picture to every store owner within 30 miles. No one knew who it was." As he spoke he reached absent mindedly for the picture to show her. "I think some of them might have recognized him, but you know how people are around here. Your business is your business." He handed the picture to Tilly. She wrinkled her brow as she searched for recognition.

"I might know who this is," she replied matter-of-factly. "He looks so familiar. I'm thinking of a guy, last winter maybe. He and his sister were coming down the mountain and it started snowing hard. Worst snow we've had in years, which isn't saying much since we don't get much down here anyway. Their truck wasn't prepared for the snow so they stopped and asked if I had a room. Luckily I did."

"Did they sign in?" Tom asked forcefully.

"Everyone signs in, Tom. Now the question is the date. I remember it was in early January, but that's about it. After dinner I'll pull out my registration books and see if I can figure it out."

Tom was incredulous. He spent the entire day roaming around the Sierras when he could have just shown Tilly before he left and been done with it. "If you do that, I'll do the dishes." Tom said.

"Done!" Tilly exclaimed, pointing a sharp finger at him.

As Tom scrubbed the dishes, Tilly went to her desk and pulled out her stack of registration ledgers. He brought them into the kitchen and placed them on the table. Since they were six-month ledgers, she found the one she needed quickly. She turned to January and after only a few minutes found the entry. Tom was just stacking the last plate when Tilly turned to him.

"The guy's name was Abel Hodges. No address, but he did list his hometown as Shafter, CA. The sister's name was Andrea. I remember she had a bad hand or something. Very pretty girl, though. I remember they were kinda peculiar. Though they were in their twenties, they acted like teenagers towards each other. Seemed very nice. Loving, but not in a weird way. Reminded me of how my brothers and I acted towards each other when we were kids. Made an impression, I guess."

"And how sure are you about the picture being him?" Tom asked.

"Pretty sure. This old lady's mind is like a steel trap!" she said, pointing to her temple.

"Good enough for me. I guess I'll be checking out in the morning," Tom stated. He took off his pink apron and hung it on its hook by the door. "Thanks, Tilly," he said walking quickly down the hall. Tilly just shook her head as she began to close down the house for the night.

Tom made it to his room and took out his computer. He lay down on his bed and searched the name "Abel Hodges Shafter CA" on the internet. He found that Abel owned Hodges Farms, a small organic farm outside Shafter. Seemed like a regular guy, 28 years old, unmarried as far as Tom could tell. There was an address for Hodges Farms. Tom mapped it and found it north of Shafter, halfway to Wasco.

Tom remembered the story Pete Zisk told him about Homer Todd, the old man who woke up in bed on his lawn. Tom navigated to Pete's website and searched for the story. In a few clicks, he found it. There was a map showing where the house had been located. Tom zoomed in on the map. He traced his finger along the screen. Less than half a mile away was Hodges Farms.

Tom let out an audible snort. *This cannot be a coincidence,* he thought. *Did Abel Hodges save him? Was Abel Hodges 'the Angel?'* His head spun with questions and he decided to find Mr. Hodges tomorrow and get some answers. As he lay there looking at the ceiling, his computer open beside him, Tom suddenly felt exhausted and laid his head back. Less than a minute later he was asleep. Had he glanced at his computer, he may have noticed the tiny LED next to its built-in webcam had turned on.

Chapter 6

In the morning, Tom ate another large breakfast with Tilly. He packed up his car and checked his phone. Still fried. He'd have to pick up another one later. He said goodbye to Tilly and by 9AM, he began his hour-long drive to Shafter. He passed the time by trying to figure out what he was going to say when he met the *man in plaid*. This was not a typical situation. *Hi, I'm Tom. You saved me last week, remember?* He hoped the words would come when he got there, because right now he wasn't coming up with anything.

Tom had no trouble finding the area Hodges Farms was located. There were not many homes in that area. What few residences were there were mostly farmhouses and a few mobile homes. Most of that part of the county was dominated by almond orchards and row crops, mostly, cotton, alfalfa, and corn.

He turned onto French Road, which supposedly dead-ended at his destination. The road was surrounded by orange groves. Though the trees looked healthy, there were many weeds, par for the course for organic crops. About half a mile down, he passed a partially burned house being worked on he believed to be Homer Todd's place. There was a mobile home sitting behind it that looked out of place. He assumed Homer was staying there while his home was being rebuilt. He saw an old man swinging a hammer nearby and decided to talk to him.

He pulled over on the dirt road and got out. The old man noticed him and walked over. He had a definite hitch on his left side, but looked more like 60 than 80.

"Morning," Tom said sticking out his hand.

"Morning, young feller," the old man replied shaking Tom's hand firmly. "Name's Homer Todd. What can I do ya for?"

"Name's Tom Salem. I'm looking for Abel Hodges."

"Abel, huh? What's this about?" the old man asked suspiciously.

"Nothing bad," Tom remarked. "I'm a reporter and I'm doing a story on local organic farms." Tom hated to lie, but the truth sounded too silly out loud.

"Oh, okay," the old man said. "If you keep headin' west, the road dead ends at his place." The old man pointed down to the road. "If he's not there, his sister probably is. You might have to yell, though. She spends more time in her garden than anywhere else."

"Thanks. I was hoping I was on the right track" Tom looked around. "Looks like you had a fire here. Was it recent?"

"Nah, sir, happened awhile back," he said. Tom could see a twinkle in the old man's eyes. "The insurance company didn't think it was worth rebuilding. Called it a total loss and gave me a check to build a new place. Well sir, they didn't understand that this house means a lot to me. Built by my granddaddy. One of the first permanent structures in this county. Over the years more than 50 children have been raised here. So, I'm rebuilding it a little a time. My grandson, Jem, helps me on the weekend. Hopefully I'll live long enough to see it whole again."

"Can't you just use the money to pay someone to repair it?" Tom asked.

"Oh yeah, it's not the money, you see, it's the meaning of it. My granddaddy built it, daddy expanded it, and I will rebuild it. My son-in-law is 'bout useless with a hammer, but he has a good son that thinks like I do. This house, well, it's a family thing, get it?"

"I do," Tom replied emphatically. It was one of the things he loved about Kern County. Family and traditions meant so much to these people. "Thank you for your help, sir." They shook hands again and they parted. He got back in his car and continued down the road.

Tom thought about the interesting dichotomy of the great Central Valley, versus the rest of California as he drove. The old man was a great example of the area. When people think of California, it's always surfers and movie stars. Most people that come here never pass this way. They spend all their time and money in Hollywood trying to find Angelina Jolie or be discovered themselves. *This is the real California*, he thought. *The part that feeds 75% of the world. The part with such strong core values.* It was people like Homer that Tom loved to write about. *Maybe I'll come back sometime and interview him*, he thought.

The big house and shop area came into view as he neared it. The orchard had obscured it right up until the end of the road. It looked like a typical small-scale family farming operation. Large house, surrounded by a little grass, open gravel-covered areas with farm implements parked in neat rows, on old truck or two nearby, and a large garage/shop area with large rolled-up doors. There was also a large, wooden sign that said Hodges Farms suspended from the eaves connected to the wrap-around porch.

Tom parked on the gravel covering the circular driveway. He got out of his car and approached the house. It was very quiet. The front of the house was decorated with a 4th of July motif even though it was a month passed. He walked up the steps and approached the door.

Just as he was about to knock, the door opened. On the other side of the security screen was an attractive young woman with light brown hair. She was likely in her late 20's and dressed in denim overalls and a white tank top.

She smiled and asked, "can I help you?" The tone was more polite than suspicious.

"Hi, ma'am. My name is Tom Salem. I'm a reporter with the Bakersfieldian."

"A reporter, huh? You're lying to me, Tom," she stated.

Tom looked bewildered. Just as he started to open his mouth with a reply, she said, "you're a columnist. There's a difference, right?" She smiled. Her tone was coy, almost playful. "I love your column! One of the few reasons I even get the paper anymore."

Tom blushed. "Thank you, ma'am. It's always nice to meet a friendly fan." Tom was befuddled. He hadn't expected to meet someone that knew who he was, let alone be a fan of his column.

"Call me Andrea, please." She unlatched the screen and opened it up. "Would you like to come in? It's awful hot out there."

"Thanks, Andrea. I'd love to."

As he walked in he was transported back 100 years. Though the house itself was obviously modern construction, the inside looked like a turn of the century farmhouse. Not rundown or dingy, just antique. It was also very clean and smelled great!

"So, Tom, to what do we owe this visit? Oh, please sit down." She motioned to the couch. Tom noticed she kept her left hand very close to her abdomen, like her stomach ached.

"Well, I really came looking for Abel. Is he around?"

"Abel? He's always around," she said. She smiled and sat down on the other end of the couch. "He'll be along directly. It's almost lunchtime and he always comes in for lunch. Have you eaten?"

"No, but I couldn't impose."

"It's no problem, I always make extra. You never know how hungry Abel will be. And anything extra always goes to the hogs. Almost Fair time, you know, and we got a couple of 4-H kids that keep their hogs out here. Just let me go set another plate." Andrea got up and went to the kitchen. As she got up from the couch, her left arm dropped and Tom saw why she kept it close to her. It was small and withered looking. It didn't look outwardly damaged, though, so possibly a birth defect.

"So, are you two married or…" Tom asked, his words trailing off. He knew they weren't married, but it opened the conversation.

"He's actually my twin brother, though you'd never tell by looking. In fact, we were born right back there in that bedroom." She pointed nonchalantly to the back of the house. "Other than when I was married, we've both been living here ever since"

"Really? I didn't think people still did that. Were your parents hippies?" he asked with a forced chuckle.

"No," she laughed. "Dad said we just came too fast to get to the hospital." Her face suddenly got a serious look to it. "Unfortunately, mom didn't make it. There were some complications and she bled to death before the ambulance got here. She got to hold us first, though." She smiled a forced smile.

"I'm sorry to hear that," Tom said, regretting the 'hippie' quip.

"Don't worry about it. Hard to miss something you never had. And our father was the most loving man you could imagine."

Tom heard boots walking on the porch outside. They stopped as they hit the front door. After a moment, it opened and in walked the *man in plaid*. He smiled at Tom and remarked loudly, "Oh, we have company."

41

"This is Tom Salem, the writer," Andrea explained from the kitchen. "He wants to talk to you about something. Give me a couple of minutes to finish up and ya'll can come to the table." She paused for a moment then added, "did you take your filthy boots off?

"Yes, Andy," he drawled.

Abel walked towards Tom and bent down towards him with is hand outstretched. He was every bit of 6'4" and his hands looked as if they could wrap around a basketball. As Tom reached to meet his hand Abel suddenly grabbed it and pulled Tom close.

"What the heck are you doing here, mister!" he quietly spat at Tom.

Tom was befuddled again. "I- I'm looking for you, I think. My name is Tom--"

"I know who you are, buddy!" Abel quietly spat. "What are you doing in my house? What do you want?" He shook Tom slightly as he asked.

"Ju-just some answers," Tom stammered out.

Abel closed his eyes and turned his head down slightly, calming himself. He forcefully whispered, "okay, okay. We're going to sit down and have lunch with my sister. She doesn't know what happened and you had better keep it that way. Make up some reason for being here and we'll talk privately afterward."

The glare in his eyes seemed to bore through Tom's head. *I hope he doesn't have heat vision,* he mused.

Andrea called for them to come in for lunch and immediately Abel's face changed to something far more jovial.

This was a man used to wearing a mask, Tom thought, *a man with something to hide.*

They sat down at the small kitchenette to a lunch of fried chicken, boiled potatoes and carrots, corn bread and salad. It was the best meal he had had in months. *Heck, maybe years*, he thought. As good as Tilly's food was, this was in a different league.

They didn't speak during the meal except to compliment the chef. Tom assumed they didn't talk while eating and he obliged them. Besides, they weren't looking at him like they were waiting for him to begin. So, he just decided to savor the meal.

As the meal neared completion, it was Andrea that spoke first. "Well, Mr. Salem, what exactly are you here about?" Andrea asked, wiping her mouth on her cloth napkin. Tom looked at Abel who was looking at his food. In fact, Tom noticed he was looking at his plate the entire time. While he was probably deep in thought, he also seemed submissive in a way. It was almost like Andrea was his mother, not his sister, the way he kept complimenting her food and even got up before her to get the missing butter dish.

"I'm doing a column on local organic farms in Kern County. As you can imagine, there are not too many. Most of the locally-grown organic produce comes from Tulare or San Luis Obispo Counties. I'm interested in seeing how your farm runs on a daily basis. How do you market your crops? How do you deal with pests? That sort of thing." In fact, Tom had been planning on doing a story on this very topic, so it wasn't a total fabrication.

"It's not easy, is it Abel?"

He shook his head.

43

"Luckily, we're a small outfit," she stated. "We don't have a lot of the overhead that large farms do. The land is paid for and so is my old truck I take to the Farmers Markets."

Abel perked up. "Why don't we go for a tour of the property? I can fill you in on a lot of the information as we go."

"Sounds good," Tom affirmed.

"Do you need help with the dishes, Andy?" Abel asked.

"Nope, you boys go for a ride and I'll tidy up. I've got some work to do in the garden if you need me later."

Abel kissed the top of her head as he got up. "Thanks, Andy." He looked at Tom. "Let's go, Mr. Salem. I've got an old electric golf cart out back we use for tours."

As the two men exited the back door, Tom was amazed at the sight of a large, luscious garden where a back yard should have been. It was easily half an acre and filled with beautiful exotic-looking trees, shrubs and small plants. They were in pots, terraces, hanging from tree branches and even raised beds. It was magnificent! It had a small greenhouse at its center that appeared to be stuffed with beautiful flowering plants.

Abel noticed Tom staring wide-eyed and remarked, "Andy, takes care of all of it. I only help with the heavy stuff. She loves gardening and the garden loves her. She's in there all the time."

They walked to an old 4-seater golf cart and got in. Abel began what sounded like a rehearsed speech, "all of this land was originally bought by my grandfather. He was the first of us Hodges in this area." Abel waved his hands around in a circle motioning to area. "He came here with my grandma shortly after World War 2. He had two sons, my father Pete and his twin brother, Paul, who died in Vietnam. Dad was the first to try organic farming in this area in the 70's. Back when it wasn't cool. He didn't get rich, but he did alright and my sister and I took it over from him when he passed a few years back."

They approached a large barn and turned down a dirt road next to it. Behind the barn was an old two-seater Cessna. Abel saw Tom eye the small plane and remarked, "I learned how to fly when I was a teenager, but never got my license. I worked for a crop duster one summer, who used to take me up in his two-seater. It flies alright, but I'd like to get my license before I put any money into it." Soon they were out of sight of the house and surrounded by orange trees. Abel stopped the cart and got out. He walked around the cart passed Tom and into the orchard. Tom followed and they stopped next to a recently dug hole.

"Alright, how did you find me?" Abel asked, not looking at Tom.

"So, it's true? You saved me?" Tom asked.

"Against my better judgment," Abel said. "I don't have a lot of sympathy for people who throw away God's greatest gift. But I also couldn't let you die knowing I could save you. That would have been a greater sin."

"How?" Tom asked. "How did you save me?"

Abel shook his head and looked off into the distance towards the house. He thought for a full minute. "You aren't going to let it go, are you? I mean, you're a reporter and that makes you a naturally curious person. No matter how hard I try to convince you to drop it, you won't, will you?"

Tom thought for a moment then replied, "Mr. Hodges, I know one thing: I owe you my life. If you tell me right now, with all sincerity, that you want me to drop it, I will leave you alone and never contact

45

you or your sister again. I always pay my debts." It was Tom's turn to stare off in the distance. "Will it gnaw at me? Absolutely, but I'll get passed it."

"Are you just looking for a story to write? I read what you wrote about your suicide attempt. People are going to expect you to be searching for answers in future columns," Abel observed.

"I meant what I said, Mr. Hodges. I won't write a thing if you don't want me to. I want to know what happened for me, not my readers. I can leave this discussion out completely. I just have to know!" Tom raised his voice for that final sentence, surprising himself.

"Abel thought for a minute, then turned to Tom. "Well," he hesitated, "I guess it's time I told someone."

Chapter 7

"Let's go over to the barn. We can sit and talk there," Abel said.

"Sounds good," Tom replied, happy to be moving away from the big hole in the ground.

Abel saw Tom glance at the hole. "Busted irrigation line," he half-laughed. The two men got into the cart and drove a short distance to the large shop. Abel drove the cart into the open doors and they parked inside. Inside were assorted tractor parts and work benches covered in small odds and ends. It was illuminated with clear roofing in spots, the large fluorescent lights hanging from the ceiling but not turned on. Abel parked the cart and then pointed to an old dinette set sitting in the corner. The two men exited the cart and sat at the old table.

"I've spent my entire life hiding what I can do. It wasn't easy growing up in a small town like Shafter. It helped that we lived way out here, but still, there were a lot of close calls." As he spoke, Abel began to stare off in the distance.

"What is it you can do exactly, Mr. Hodges?" Tom asked.

Abel got up and walked over to a large farm implement. He reached down with one hand and picked it up over his head. Tom figured the large piece of iron weighed over 1,000 pounds. It was an unreal display considering how easy he made it look. Tom stared with his mouth open. Abel put it down gently and sat back down.

"How strong are you?" Tom asked.

"Really, I don't know. I've never found anything I couldn't lift. I've lifted cars, tractors, boulders, trees….none of it gave me much trouble. The strength makes it easy for me to run pretty fast and jump real high. That's how I saved you."

Tom was thoughtful for a moment. He was processing a lot of new information. "So, you were at the bottom of the cliff and saw me step off?"

"Yeah, I go up there almost every weekend. I have to exercise my muscles or else they get very tight and achy. I think it's kinda like when you sit in one place too long, then get up. You have to stretch. At least that's what Andy tells me. Anyway, I was just getting ready to go when I saw you up there through the branches. You stepped off, I jumped up and caught you. That's probably when your ribs got hurt. I didn't have time to be gentle. My momentum carried us into the cliff-side, and then we dropped. You had passed out. I jumped back up to the top and put you in your car. Luckily, there were a few rocky ledges for me to bounce off of since I couldn't jump that high in one leap. Then I called for an ambulance. I waited until I saw them coming up, then jumped back down and ran to my truck."

Tom was listening and imagining it happening. It all made perfect sense, but still sounded crazy out loud. But after what he just saw Abel do, it was certainly an acceptable explanation. Tom stood and walked around thinking for a moment.

"It just occurred to me I haven't thanked you. Thanks for saving me," Tom said without looking at him.

"Like I said, Tom, I had to. It was the Christian thing to do," Abel intoned.

"You said Andy told you what muscle achiness was like. Andy isn't strong like you?" Tom asked. "You're twins, right?"

"We are twins, but this thing that makes me different, it's probably genetic. Dad had it, too. Andy is actually the first girl born in our family in generations. Dad used to say it was a Y-chromosome thing, but we don't really know."

"Your Dad, huh? How about grandpa?"

"Never met him. He and grandma had passed away years before I was born. Wish I had known them, though. Apparently, they met during the war when grandpa helped liberate a concentration camp. Grandma was a gypsy they had locked up for being 'undesirable'. They fell in love, got married and moved back to good ol' Shafter. Grandma died a few years later of some type of cancer. Grandpa died of a heart attack in the 70's."

"How about your uncle Paul? He wasn't like you and your dad?" Tom asked.

"Yeah, he was, but even we have our limits. I guess the enemy found his. They never told dad how he died and dad never saw the body. The funeral director said the body was pretty badly burned. We figured it was napalm. Our skin is tough, but not completely fireproof. Takes a lot to burn it, but eventually it does burn."

"And your dad?" Tom asked.

"A heart attack!" yelled a female voice from the rolled-up door.

Abel and Tom both jumped and turned to see Andrea standing there with a very serious look on her face. She had one hand on her hip, the other clung to her side.

"Andy…" Abel started to say something, but was cut off.

Andrea waved her hand and dropped her head. "DARN it, Abel. We work so hard to keep your secret and of all people, you tell a reporter? Why would you do this to us?"

49

"I'm sorry, Andy. I just get tired of keeping it all in. We've talked about it before…"

"We've talked about you sharing this with a therapist! Someone who is sworn to keep secrets! And it was just talk! We have sacrificed so much to keep you safe…." She whimpered the last bit, on the edge of sobbing.

"Ms. Hodges, Andrea, I assure you I can keep a secret." Tom stammered the words out, hoping to reassure her.

"No offense, Tom, but dishing on the public is how you make a living. Wouldn't revealing the existence of a 'superhuman' in a small town increase circulation? Ad revenue? How about in 5 years when the internet has completely killed print journalism? Will the Bakersfieldian need a huge story to save it and your job? Will you be there with the story of a lowly farmer who can leap tall cliffs in a single bound? And by the way, my last name isn't Hodges. It's Wilson!"

Tom thought for a minute, then his eyes turned down. Was she a widow? If she lost a husband at such a young age, the thought of losing her brother was unfathomable. "Andrea, would it help you feel better if you knew something about me? Something so shameful it would be the end of my career if it came out?"

The fire in her eyes began to subside. "What are you talking about?" she asked skeptically.

"Abel has shared something very private with me regarding him and your family. If it came out, well, I don't know what would happen but your lives would change forever and probably not for the better. To ensure I never say anything, I will give you a secret about me that no one knows, not even my ex-wife. If it came out, I would be completely ostracized and rightly so."

Andrea had completely calmed down. She stared at him intently and her eyes went from anger to concern. Andrea was obviously a very giving and compassionate soul, Tom thought, to make that transition so quickly. She reluctantly sat down at the table, taking Abel's hand.

"What do you know about the accident I was involved in two years ago?"

"Tom, you don't need to…." Andrea started.

"Yeah, I do," Tom said. "Please, tell me what you know."

Andrea thought for a moment. "Well, I know your daughter, Gwen was her name I think, her school bus was involved in a car accident in the canyon on the way back from Tehachapi. You were on the bus, too. The bus went off the road and overturned. It hung off the side of the canyon." She paused. "Your daughter fell through an open window." Tom's eyes began to fill with tears. He hadn't allowed the name to enter his mind for well over a year. He fought them back.

"I was chaperoning the trip. The kids were so excited. It had been the first time some of these kids had been to a forest. Can you imagine that? Anyway, I was sitting next to her on the bus. As we came around a corner, there was a large boulder in the road, they fall all the time, but the bus driver overcorrected and we rolled over on our side, sliding to the edge. It was a miracle the whole bus didn't just fall off into the river. The back of the bus swung over the side. Most weren't wearing seat belts and ended up scattered around the bus. Gwenie….," he choked at saying her name. "Gwenie ended up on top of a side window. The glass was broken but still in place. When my mind cleared, I saw her laying there, her eyes wide and scared as she looked down and looked at me. I started to crawl to her and the windows beneath me began to crack. There was no other way to her. The seats were blocking the way. I…froze." Tom paused again, looking down at the table.

Andrea and Abel both looked horrified. Tom continued, "every movement I made, even my heartbeat, caused the window to 'spider web' a little more. I was…paralyzed…with fear. I looked down and saw the rocks below. I looked up at Gwenie. One second she was there. I blinked and she was gone. She screamed for me the whole way down." Tom shuddered and fought his sobs. "My sudden movement broke through the glass and my top half fell through. I tried to scramble through it the rest of the way, go after Gwenie, but the bus driver grabbed me. He had been saving the kids by crawling across the bench seats, pulling them out 2-3 at a time. He got them all out and then he got to the back and kept me from doing the most obvious thing: dying with my daughter."

Andrea reached across the table for Tom's hand. "It wasn't your fault, Tom." She and Abel both had tears in their eyes.

"That is what the bus driver said. That is what everyone says. But they didn't see me freeze. In those seconds, I could have made it to Gwenie! I could have moved her from the glass!" Tom shook his head. "But I froze. And she is dead because of it. My daughter, my grandchildren, everything she would ever be, gone because I was a coward."

Andrea moved to Tom and embraced him. He returned the embrace and shuddered in her arms. He wept for what felt like an eternity, but was just a few minutes. When he looked up, there was a box of tissue in front of him. He took a few and wiped his face. He noticed Abel sat with his eyes closed. The slight movement of his lips suggested to Tom that he might be praying.

Tom cleared his throat. "I fought the bus drivers' attempts to save me so he knocked me out and pulled me over the seats and out of the bus. He was a real hero that day. I got put on suicide watch at Kern Medical for a week. Over the months, I learned to block it all out so I could survive. I couldn't even think her name until recently.

My wife handled it better than me but, as you know, my marriage fell apart. I was a shell. Tanya was an incredible woman and she certainly deserved better than me. I really tried to make her the bad guy in my mind. Her looks of concern I rationalized into looks of disgust. Her desire to help me became a desire to be away from me. She never blamed me but the blame I put on myself I attributed to her. It was me that filed for divorce. She fought it for a while but how long can you really fight it? I knew I would die as soon as the divorce was finalized. I prepared for it. And you know the rest."

Abel stood up and paced a bit. Andrea still held both of Tom's hands with her good one. Abel turned to look at them. "Tom, I don't think you were a coward. I think you hesitated. We all hesitate. Even I hesitated before I saved you. Unfortunately, this one hesitation cost you everything. I won't even pretend to understand what you are going through. But I know that hesitation, well." Abel looked to Andrea. "Andy, how do you feel about all this?"

"I'm so sorry for you, Tom," Andrea stated sympathetically. "I can't imagine how hard it was to tell us that. You've managed to keep that secret. I guess we can trust you with ours."

Andrea stood up and announced, "I've got some cookies baking. How about I bring them and some iced tea back in a few minutes? You fellas can keep talking. I'll catch up when I get back."

"Thanks," they both said almost in unison.

As she walked away, Tom began to speak. "Do you mind if I ask you a few more questions? I'm just curious about a few things."

"Shoot," Abel replied.

"You mentioned your dad died from a heart attack. Not to be morbid, but how did they prepare the body for burial?"

"He died right here in the shop. I think he went fast because I only left him for a few minutes and when I came back, he was gone. His hand was clutched at his chest. When the ambulance got here, he was cold so they called the coroner to pick his body up instead. He was pronounced dead and they examined him and said it was a heart attack. They asked if we wanted an autopsy and I told them our religion didn't allow for the body to be cut open. We just say that to get out of vaccines and blood tests and such. Could you imagine what would happen if they had tried to give me a vaccination as a kid and they kept breaking the needles on my skin?" Both men smiled at the thought.

It feels good to smile, Tom thought.

"The coroner took him straight to the funeral home. We had him cremated. Like I said, our skin is tough, but it'll burn if you heat it up enough. I imagine it took a little longer than usual, but not enough for the funeral home people to say anything to us about it. We spread his ashes in Andy's garden."

"Seems like things fell into place, you know, outside of losing your dad."

"Well, we had spent a lot of time talking about it growing up. Just a quick discussion or two when I was real young. Then, I got the flu really bad once and dad nearly took me in to the ER when it turned to pneumonia. I begged him not to. I got better and then our discussions got more serious after that. No hospitals for either of us, no matter what."

Andrea returned with the tea and cookies. How she managed to carry the tray with one hand and not spill anything amazed Tom. They sat and ate the cookies and drank the tea. Abel and Andrea told stories about close calls they had keeping Abel's secret. Before long, Tom noticed it getting darker outside and knew it was time to call it a day.

"Well, I guess I better be off. I haven't been home in a few days and I'm sure people are looking for me." He took one last pull off the ice tea glass and finished it.

"You could stay for supper. I'm making chili beans," Andrea offered.

"No, I'm sure I need to check in with my boss. I've been out of touch for three days now and my cell phone broke. I've got an old one at home I can use but I have to have it activated. Since I don't have a landline at home and no access to my voicemail, I'm completely out of the loop."

"Okay," Andrea replied, "but you just remember, Tom, you are family now. Our secrets bind us together. You are welcome to come by anytime." She hugged him.

"I'll walk you to your car," Abel offered.

"Thanks," Tom replied. They walked the 100 yards to Tom's car as Andrea walked towards the house.

"Are you heading up to the woods this weekend?" Tom asked.

"Yeah," Abel affirmed.

"Would you mind if I went with you?"

Abel smiled. "You want to see what I can really do, huh?" he asked.

"Yeah," Tom said.

55

"I would love the company. I'll see if Andy wants to come along. There are a few shops up there she likes to go to and a great cafe we can have lunch at."

"Sounds like fun," Tom mused. They shook hands and Tom got in the car and began to amble down the long road, oblivious to the dusty El Camino parked two rows into the orchard as he passed.

Chapter 8

Back home was just as Tom figured. Tanya had left a note on his door to call her, but at least she wasn't staked out there. He found his old phone and quickly activated it. He called his boss and let him know he was okay and would be back the following Monday. He took his laptop out and began to file through the messages.

A lot of readers were still sending him supportive messages. So were co-workers and friends. It was nice to read and he tried to respond to them all. Tanya had emailed him a few dozen times, her messages showing an increasing sign of agitation. He knew he should contact her, but just didn't feel he could yet.

Just then, there was a knock at the door. Tom thought about not answering it but thought better. He knew it was Tanya before he even got to the door. He opened it up and there she was.

"Your mom taught you better than this, you jerk!" she spat, trying to remain calm. Tanya had loved Tom's mom and it really affected her when she had passed the year before Gwen.

"You are right, as usual," Tom replied snarkily.

Tanya didn't wait to be asked inside. She walked passed Tom, saying, "I'm glad you decided to come home. Now maybe you can explain to me what the heck you were thinking."

Not bothering to be coy, Tom said, "I was thinking I would be dead and not have to answer any more questions from you."

"You may have forced the divorce, Tomcat, but you cannot force me to stop caring about you." She always called him Tomcat when she was mad at him.

"You're right, again. Feel better?" Tom didn't actually feel the need to be so mean, but it was a habit when talking with her now. He forced himself to tone it down. "I'm sorry," he said, breathing a big sigh, "I should have contacted you before I left town. I'm really am sorry I worried you."

"Where did you go?"

"To Tilly's to sleep. Prowled around the mountain looking for answers during the day." Tom wasn't about to tell her about Abel.

Tanya looked him in the eye. "Did you find any answers?"

"I think so. I think the answer is to stop being a jerk to those that care about me and move on with my life. I should be dead, but somehow, I'm not. Maybe I didn't even jump. Maybe it was all a dream."

"From what your dad says, it may have been a hallucination. You never were much of a drinker." She looked concerned as she spoke to him. She moved her hand to the side of his cheek.

Tom backed away from her touch and turned away. "Either way, I'm passed it. Just being near death, real or imagined, has changed my perspective." Tom gazed out his kitchen window. "I miss her, Tanya. I still miss her so much."

Tanya moved to him and embraced him from behind. She squeezed him hard. "So do I," she whispered.

After a short embrace, Tom turned to face her. "But that's not why I did it. I need to tell you about that day. I need to tell you exactly what happened and hope that you don't hate me as much as I hate myself."

Tom proceeded to tell Tanya about the wreck, this time not holding back anything. He spoke of his cowardice and seeing his little girl plunge to her death. He spoke of his desire to join her and being stopped by the bus driver. He spoke of how the guilt drove a wedge between them he could never remove. Even now he imagined disgust in her eyes when there was only concern.

When he finished his story, Tanya stared at him, mouth agape. She turned and sat in his recliner. "You've been dealing with that all this time," she said, more a statement than a question.

"Do you hate me?" he asked.

Tanya hesitated. "No, Tom, I could never hate you. But I'm not exactly happy with you. We were married. You should have shared this pain with me. I could have helped you through it. Instead, you shut down in your self-pity at a time when we should have been closest. You didn't fail Gwen, Tomcat, you failed me."

Tom looked up at her, eyes narrowed in confusion.

"You were selfish," she pointed out with an obvious irritation in her voice. "You took the part of you I needed to help me heal and you hid it away from the light. And what's worse, you denied me my right as your wife to share the burden of your pain. That is what we swore to do."

They didn't speak for a full minute. Then, Tanya spoke first, "I still love you, Tom. That hasn't changed."

"I still love you, too," he said. They embraced, but not passionately. There was resignation. They were divorced and that would not be changing. *Maybe we could be friends again, someday,* Tom thought.

They spoke for another hour or so. Mostly, they talked about what was going on in their lives. Tanya explained she had been spending more time with her elderly parents. They had introduced her to their tax attorney and the two had been on several dates. He couldn't really blame her and sincerely hoped for the best for her. He told her he would start seeing a therapist soon. Then she left.

For the first time in a long while, Tom felt good. He was optimistic about life and was looking forward to starting his next article. Writing about his reason for being suicidal was going to be emotionally brutal, but it would be therapeutic. He would undoubtedly receive a lot of support from concerned friends and family and fans. More importantly, his revelations would more than likely throw people off the idea of him being "saved" by something that night. Most will write it off as him having a vivid imagination in a drunken stupor. It would throw off any suspicion of Abel, the Angel of Kern County.

Chapter 9

Three Months Later

       Abel, Sam, and Andrea were in the front seat of Abel's old blue truck heading up the mountain. It was a roomy cab, but their winter clothes made them appear squished together. Even though he didn't get cold, Abel still wore his cold weather gear.

After a long pause in the conversation, Tom was the first to speak. "So, Abel, are you coming up to town or are we dropping you off at your spot?" Tom asked.

       "You guys can drop me off at the 'exercise yard' and I'll meet you for lunch. How about that little place in Ponderosa?" Abel asked.

       "How far is that from your spot?" Tom asked.

       "I'm guessing about 20 miles the way I'll be going. Lots of trees and boulders along the way. I should get a good workout," Abel said with enthusiasm.

       "Awesome!" exclaimed Andrea. "I want to visit that antique store in Kernville afterward but we can go to the Farmers Market in Camp Nelson first."

       "Do they still have that when it's this cold?" Tom asked.

       "Farmers work in all weather, Tom," she stated coyly.

When they reached the pullout above Abel's 'exercise yard' he and Tom got out in order to switch places. Abel bounded down the side of the mountain. He would spend 15 or so minutes searching for trail cams, but would wear his balaclava the whole time anyway. He had a thick white jacket and white snow pants to help him blend in. He and Tom had actually spent a lot of time discussing what he could do to stay incognito. Abel took many more precautions than he used to.

Tom got back in the warm truck on the driver side. He slowly moved forward so he didn't slide on the snow. It wasn't very deep on the side of the road, and non-existent on the road itself, but he didn't like to take chances. People from Bakersfield just weren't used to cold weather driving.

Andrea did not move over the to the passenger side when Tom got in. While they weren't 'together' officially, they had grown very close in the months they had known each other. Tom came out to the ranch nearly every Friday for game night, and came along most Saturdays for Abel's exercise. The siblings often managed to bring him to church services on Sunday morning. Tom had even been allowed to help Andrea in her precious garden more than once.

When they reached the Farmer's Market, they pulled off the road. Most of the booths had large propane heaters next to their fare. *It was actually quite pleasant*, Tom thought. Though there were a lot fewer booths this time of year, the two spent more than an hour walking around, inspecting and sampling different foods and produce and admiring the local crafts. Andrea studied a particular necklace very hard, almost transfixed by it for more than a minute, then quickly put it back. After she moved on, Tom picked it up. It seemed pretty, but unremarkable. It was a simple blue stone surrounded by a Native American wind catcher design. Still, she was so intent on it she must have liked it. Tom quickly bought it, out of Andrea's view, and stuck the small box containing it into his jacket.

They ended up buying a few things together and walked back to the truck to stow their packages in the cab. They decided to walk the small trail next to the market just to stretch their legs. The path was wooded, but flat with only a powdering of snow. After a quarter mile, the two stopped at a bench to admire the view of the white Sierras.

Tom decided it was time to give Andrea the gift he had just purchased. He took the box out of his pocket and handed it to Andrea.

"What's this?" she asked.

"I noticed you admiring it at the market. I figured anything that you stared at like that must be important to you in some way," Tom said.

Andrea put the box on her lap and used her good hand opened it. She immediately put her fingertips to her mouth. "Oh, Tom," she began weakly. She stared at the necklace for a few seconds and then replaced the top. She looked up and off into the distance.

"We've never talked about my ex-husband, have we?" she asked.

Tom was wary. The necklace obviously brought back some memory of her husband. Tom wasn't sure he wanted her to have those memories. "No, we haven't," he replied simply. Other than Andrea having the last name Wilson, the two never brought him up.

"His name was Rex. Rex Wilson, obviously. He was Abel's best friend growing up. He lived a few ranches over, not far as the crow flies. The three of us were inseparable. He spent so much time at our house I think it was just expected we would fall in love. And we did. Madly, in fact, once we were old enough to know what that type of love was. We were married right out of high school and his family built us a small house on their property. For a time, we were very happy." Her voice began to shake but she caught it.

"Andrea, you don't have to tell me anything you're not comfortable with." Tom took her good hand and put it in his. She kept her withered hand in her pocket. 'We're friends, good friends. I don't want you to..."

She cut him off. "Tom, I think we are more than friends. Or at least, I see us heading that way. I don't want any weirdness between us. Besides, it's no secret." She squeezed Tom's hand and continued. "Rex's family wasn't as religious as ours. They weren't bad people, mind you, just a little more outgoing and worldly than we were. They would have big BBQ's at their house and the alcohol flowed freely. Don't get me wrong, Abel and I enjoy the occasional drink, but never to the point of becoming drunk. And Rex was like that, too, at first. But it's an old story, I'm afraid. He went from drinking a little at the family get-togethers, to drinking a little each day, to getting drunk a few times a week. He was always such a sweet guy but that bottle just brought out something different, something angry. One day, the anger boiled over and he hit me. Not very hard, but it left a bruise around my eye. It's a cliché, but he was so nice afterward. He cried and cried and doted on me for the rest of the night. Even made me breakfast the next morning. It may have been enough to turn him around, but unfortunately for him, Abel came by that morning."

Tom's eyebrows rose. "Let me guess, Abel took matters into his own hand?"

Andrea clenched her eyes shut. "I've never seen Abel so mad. Not in his entire life, before or since. As soon as he figured out what happened, he lit out after Rex so fast he exploded the kitchen door off its hinges and into pieces. Rex was driving a tractor half a mile away and Abel was running so fast he tore right through it instead of slowing down. I followed in my pickup and by the time I got there he had ripped the cab off and had Rex raised up in the air by his neck. I screamed at Abel to drop him as he pulled his fist back. I could tell Abel was fighting hard not to kill him. Rex's eyes were bulging out of

64

their sockets and he was turning blue. I guess his sense won over his anger and he dropped him. I ran to Rex on the ground. He was breathing and his color returned. Abel hadn't broken anything, but he was pretty roughed up."

Tom asked, "Rex didn't know about Abel's abilities?"

"No," Andrea said. "Rex knew he was as strong as a bull and tough as nails. Used to give him crap about not joining the football team in high school, but he had no idea about just how strong and tough Abel was until that day. Next thing I knew Abel bent down and looked Rex in the face, eye to eye. He told him to leave town, leave me, leave everything and go or I would not save him next time. Abel walked away and I guess out of frustration slammed his fist into the pickup, smashing the whole front end."

"So, he left? Just like that?"

"Yeah, I mean within a couple of days. He told his family he was tired of living here and I wasn't willing to leave, so he was leaving me. He took some money we had saved out of the bank. Then he left."

"Didn't anyone think it was weird, the truck and tractor being all busted up?" Tom asked.

"We told people Rex had run into the tractor. Rex's parents figured he was drunk when it happened. I got the divorce on grounds of abandonment. Then I moved back home."

"And he hasn't come back or contacted you since then?" Tom asked.

"If you had seen the look in Abel's eyes and the state of the tractor, you wouldn't come back either," she said matter-of-factly. She paused for a second, then continued, "Rex was a good man at heart. He loved our family deeply. I'm sure he was ashamed as much as he was

65

scared of Abel. He couldn't look me in the eye the whole time he was preparing to leave." She looked down at the box and smiled. "The blue gem is the same color as his eyes."

Tom gave her a gentle sideways hug as they sat on the bench. The two stared at the powder-covered Sierras for a few more minutes before Andrea finally spoke. "Well, we better be getting to lunch. It'll probably take us some time to get up to Ponderosa with these roads." As she spoke, she stood up quickly and slapped Tom playfully on his leg.

They walked back down the path towards the truck. Tom opened Andrea's door and she got in. He hopped into the driver seat and started the car. He let it warm for a few minutes before moving out on the road and up the mountain. The truck meandered along the road for a while as the two listened to old country music on a CD player.

They finally reached the diner in Ponderosa a half hour later. The roads had been very wet from melting snow with a little black ice in the shadows of the trees. Tom was unaccustomed to driving under real winter conditions as it never snowed in Bakersfield, so he drove slowly. The diner wasn't too busy as it wasn't a very well-traveled road in the winter. Most of the patrons were locals as the diner pulled triple duty as a diner, a bar and a market.

Tom and Andrea found a booth and ordered some hot chocolate. They decided to wait to order food until Abel arrived. From their booth, they could see the bridge that ran over the Tule River, the path Abel was taking. As they sipped their hot chocolate, Tom was deep in thought. His next question wasn't meant to be out loud, but it was.

"What about Abel?" he asked.

Andrea looked at him with an eyebrow raised. "Huh?" she asked.

"Was Abel ever married?" Tom asked. He was surprised the thought had never occurred to him prior.

Andrea thought for a moment then got a sad look on her face. "No, Abel has never married."

"Why? Is he afraid of marriage?" Tom asked.

"Our father never intended to marry. Frankly, he was worried about hurting a woman when they, you know, were together." Andrea blushed. "He also worried about children. Would they be like him, would they be deformed or would he even be able to have children?" When she said 'deformed' Tom started to glance at her withered hand, but stopped himself. "When he met my mom, he tried like heck to stay away, but she pursued him pretty hard, at least according to dad. I guess she was a real pistol, but it turned out dad was right. She died during childbirth. She bled to death from the damage caused by Abel's birth, most likely."

Tom understood and didn't ask for clarification. He knew baby's bodies are supposed to compress during delivery, but Abel was probably very strong even then. Tom shuddered imagining the pain their mother had endured.

"So, Abel stays away from women because he is afraid what happened to your mom might happen to them?"

"Most likely. We've never really talked about it at length," Andrea lamented.

They both continued sipping their hot chocolate. As they waited, they took advantage of the diners' free Wi-Fi to check emails and messages. Cell service was generally very spotty on the mountain and it was only near public establishments like the diner where you could at least get a signal through Wi-Fi.

As Tom was reading an email from his editor, a message popped up. It was from Abel and it read:

Can you guys please meet me back at the spot?

Andrea looked up just then with a quizzical look on her face. "I got it, too," Tom said. He replied:

Why?

After a few minutes, the reply came:

It's important. Please get there as quickly as possible. Tell Andy to buy me a cheap jacket at the diner. I'll explain after you pick me up. If you see police, keep driving and I'll meet you at that gas station in Springville.

Tom looked at Andrea, who had moved over next to him on the booth bench seat. He replied:

Sure, might take a while to get down there, but we'll try to hurry.

Tom and Andrea picked up their stuff and paid for their drinks. They walked into the market side of the diner and found a fleece coat with *Ponderosa, CA* printed on it for tourists. Though it was way overpriced, Tom bought it and they quickly got into the truck. Tom pulled out onto the road started down the mountain, quickly but deliberately. Within 10 minutes, they had passed the Farmer's Market. They noticed a Ranger truck parked there with its lights flashing along with a few more cars that weren't there before.

They reached the spot a few minutes later and pulled off the road. Tom got out and looked around. He didn't want to shout in case there were others around. After a minute or so, Abel came walking up the side of the mountain, looking around hesitantly.

Tom walked towards him and was surprised to see him wearing only his snow pants and boots. His shirt, jacket, balaclava and beanie were missing. As he got closer, he saw a large swath of his hair was gone, too.

"What the heck is going on, Abel?"

"Are there any cars you can see?" Abel asked.

"No," Tom replied.

"Good, let's go! Quick!" Abel said moving very fast towards the passenger door.

Both men got in the truck and Abel instructed, "drive, Tom, but don't make it look obvious that you are trying to get away."

"What do you mean 'get away?'" Tom said pulling out on the road.

Abel put the jacket on and zipped it up to his neck. He then reached behind the seat and found one of his many work hats and put it on. He chuckled lightly and declared, "Well, today I finally answered a question I have had for years."

"What's that?" Andrea asked.

"Am I bulletproof?" Abel replied. "And the answer is …yes!"

Both Andrea and Tom's eyes widened. Before Tom could say anything, Andrea asked, "oh my goodness, Abel, what did you do?" As she said this she started picking up the jacket to see his skin underneath. Abel resisted.

"I'm okay, Andy, not a scratch. But I can't say the same for my clothes."

"What happened?" Tom asked. He kept his eyes on the road as he negotiated the mountain curves.

"About an hour ago I was moving up the river, having fun with it, jumping from boulders to trees, all that stuff. Then I heard a shotgun go off not too far away. I climbed up a tree to see if I could see where it came from. There was a small group of guys that had a bear cub cornered near some large rocks. They were firing different kinds of rifles near it, not trying to hit it I'm guessing, but to scare it. Maybe they wanted momma bear to come so they could harvest her. The sound of the small cub wailing was too much. I had to do something." Abel looked out the window and smiled.

"What did you do, Abel?" Andrea asked with stern suspicion in her voice.

"I know it wasn't the smartest thing to do, Andy," Abel clarified, patting her on the leg. "I jumped from tree to tree until I was near them. Then I jumped down in front of one of them. He was very stunned and as he fell backwards, his shotgun went off, tearing the jacket off my right side. I think it was birdshot. I felt it but it was only enough to knock me off balance. Well, the other guys were startled by the shot and turned to face us. I guess they thought I was the momma bear with my thick shirt and big jacket hanging off and I was bent over trying to catch my balance. They all opened fire. Twenty-two's, .308's, even shotgun slugs were bouncing off me and tearing the rest of my jacket and shirt away. I won't lie; I felt the slugs quite a bit. Luckily, I was facing them so I didn't lose my drawers, although I'm sure there are a few holes in them."

Andrea had her hand over her mouth, stunned into silence. She pulled his hat off and looked at the swaths of missing hair, rubbing his head.

70

"I think a few of the slugs grazed my head and took some hair with them," he chuckled.

"Holy crap, Abel!" Tom said loudly.

"I know," Abel chuckled in reply. "I can't ever remember being so scared there at the beginning. They opened up on me for at least 30 seconds. Then they just stopped. The impacts had knocked me clear to the ground, so I played dead. A few crept towards me, and that's when I struck. Oh, I was very careful not to let them see my face. I'm sure I moved too fast. I hit them hard enough to knock them down, but not enough to leave anything permanent. I bent their gun barrels and hung them on a high tree. They'll never reach them, but they could definitely see them. A couple of them were scrambling up a trail out of the canyon, going for help."

Tom laughed. "Sounds like they got what they had coming to them."

"I can't stand jerks with guns. Makes all gun owners look bad. And I hate bullies even more. Unfortunately, as I turned to leave, momma bear showed up. She was charging through the brush very fast and since I was the only one standing, she ran at me. I didn't want to hurt her, but I didn't want the idiots to get hurt either. So, I ran at the cub and scooped it up. It was pretty small, so I carried it away from them. Momma bear followed me and after a few hundred yards, I sat the cub down. I went back to check on the idiots and there was a Ranger there already. They were all on their feet so I moved up the river until I got near the diner at Ponderosa. Then I realized I wasn't wearing a shirt and if people saw me walking out of the woods in this weather they would definitely remember me. I checked my phone and it had survived the barrage in my hip pocket and I was close enough to the diner to use the Wi-Fi so I texted you."

"So, you were right by us when you texted?" Tom asked.

"Yeah, so close, yet so far." Abel replied. "Andy, what do you think?"

Andrea was quiet for a minute. "Abel, you have got to stop taking chances like this! Did you check for game cameras? If they were hunting, they could be using them. Could you be sure no one saw you? I hate bullies, too, but it was just a bear. You are worth more than that!" She was fuming.

Tom didn't want to get between them. He could see both sides of the argument. Abel could help and his conscious only reinforced his desire to do so. But Abel was all Andrea had and if he was discovered, she worried she would never see him again.

Abel spoke very measured words. "Andy, if that momma bear had come before I did, those men would all be dead now. I saved the cub, but I also saved six men. You know what the Word says about that, right? If I let someone die that I could save? Would the Good Samaritan have done that? "

Andy relied, "You're right, Abel, I know. Still, if you are going to take chances like this, we need a way of disguising you, so no one can see your face."

"Like a mask," Abel asked.

"You were wearing a mask. The bullets shredded it. That won't work," Andrea pointed out.

"I could make a metal helmet. I've got some inch-thick steel in the shop. I could bend it into the shape of my head." As he said it, Abel moved his hands as if he was bending metal between them.

"You gonna carry a metal helmet in your back pocket, Abel?" Andrea quipped. "And besides, the bullets might ricochet off and hit someone."

Tom chimed in, "What if it was made of something strong but flexible. Something like Kevlar. It's what cops wear. Of course, they wear a lot of layers to stop bullets. You just need a few layers that won't tear easily since your skin stops the bullets."

"Isn't that stuff really thick?" Andrea asked.

"No, it's like regular fabric. Thick, like burlap, I think, but relatively flexible. You can even use Kevlar thread to sew it together. Shoot, I bet you can get it through Amazon.com." Tom thought for a second. "I could order it for you so it can't be traced to you."

"I think we should try it, Andy. What do you think?" Abel asked.

"Hey, I'm always looking for a reason to sew. This would be my first mask, though. Better order extra in case I mess it up," Andrea said with some seriousness. "I wonder if the fabric store sells patterns for masks?"

Chapter 10

Four Months Later

The holidays came and went and soon it was early Spring. Tom had given Abel a roll of Kevlar fabric and thread for Christmas and Andrea sewed a couple of masks for him. He kept one in his back pocket. If he accidently fell out, it looked like a black handkerchief. On many Friday and Saturday nights, he would patrol the rooftops and shadows of downtown Shafter or Wasco. He had stopped a few fights and assaults. He kept a few drunks from driving by punching holes in their tires when he saw them leave the bar. He was getting very good at being 'stealthy.'

On a few occasions, he made the drive to Bakersfield to patrol their downtown area. He liked it because it felt more like a 'big city,' though it wasn't really. Downtown Bakersfield was bisected by Chester Ave with the newer, trendier bars and restaurants mostly on the west side while the east side hosted older, seeder establishments and transient hotels. On most nights, there were more people on the west side mostly due to it being cleaner, brighter and many of the bars and nightclubs were within a short walk of each other. There were numerous multi-story buildings scattered around and that made it easier for Abel to stay unseen.

Abel decided that Saint Patrick's Day would be a good time to patrol downtown Bakersfield again. With so many bars in one small area he could probably prevent a lot of people from fighting or driving drunk. He parked his truck on top of a public parking garage about 9pm and sat in it until he was sure there was no one around. The top of the parking garage was fifty feet from the top of an adjacent 3-story building. He chose this part of the garage because he and Tom had scoped it out and found no cameras focused on it.

Abel got out of his truck and locked it. He took a look around then quickly sprinted across the garage and leapt over to the 3-story building next door. From his back pocket he produced a small, black bag and put his wallet and keys in it, then stashed the bag under the building ledge. He then made his way from roof to roof until he found one where he was overlooking most of downtown. From this vantage point he could see most of Chester Ave. and a few side streets.

Drunken revelers were difficult for Abel. Often times what looked and sounded like trouble was just people having a 'good time' and several times he had stopped what he thought were sexual assaults but turned out to be anything but. A few 'fights' turned out to be horseplay. So, he didn't spring into action unless he was very sure he was needed and never in full sight of people. If there were too many people around, he would throw a rock at a nearby window and break it so the alarms would go off, making everyone run. He even had a pair of binoculars hidden on top of one of the taller buildings so he could see the people below easier.

His 'uniform' was all black sweats, black shoes and socks, and of course his Kevlar mask. He had also taken to wearing gloves used on punching bags. They had some padding across the back in case he hit anyone too hard, but still dexterous enough to use his hands and left no fingerprints.

From his vantage point, he could see there was a lot of activity. Hundreds of people milled about going from bar to bar. Most were loud, but happy. He saw a few different fights begin, but were quickly stopped by security guards and onlookers. By 10:00PM, he was sure he wouldn't be needed. He hadn't counted on the bar owners bringing in extra security for the evening.

He decided to leave his perch and check out some other areas with fewer people. Abel usually didn't go to the east side because he figured the people found in that area knew what they were in for and, frankly, they creeped him out. Still, tonight he decided they might need his watchful eye.

Unfortunately, he had to get across Chester Ave and its six lanes of slow traffic. He could just take off his mask and gloves and walk across, but he had a personal rule against it. Once the mask went on, it wouldn't come off—too many cameras, both seen and unseen. If someone described him in his mask, the authorities might be able to find him on camera from some other part of downtown based on his other clothes. He could wear a long coat, but in Bakersfield, any time of year, a long coat sticks out like a sore thumb.

So, he decided to jump across. It wasn't the distance that gave him pause. If he got a running jump, the distance was no problem. It was the landing that concerned him. Many of these old buildings had roofs in ill repair and at the speed he would be moving, he worried about damaging them when he landed. Even worse, he worried he might fall through. The short 20-30 foot jumps he normally did were no big deal, but this was a lot further and he would have a much greater impact.

Abel looked around and found two 5 story buildings on opposite sides of the road. They were both old but looked like they had been renovated in the last 20 years. Also, it appeared they were both pretty flat on top for his takeoff and landing. Below, there were about two dozen people standing around but not looking up. He backed up, got a running start, and leaped high and far. As he landed, he tried to bend his legs to absorb the impact a little bit, but heard an audible 'thunk' as he landed. If anyone was inside, they had to have heard and might be coming to investigate. He quickly moved to the adjacent roof top, then another.

After a few minutes of scanning the area, he heard a group of voices a few blocks away and decided to check it out. He leaped from rooftop to rooftop until he was atop a one-story building overlooking an alley. Below him was a group of six homeless men. They were standing in a semi-circle as two people were obviously rolling around and fighting in the middle. Abel rolled his eyes, believing it to be a dispute over drugs or something. He had seen this before and usually just a quick yell from the shadows made people scatter.

He looked closer and noticed another person, not part of the circle, lying off to the side. He looked at the pair in the center of the circle and realized it was a man and a woman. At that moment, the man smashed hard against the woman's temple with his fist and she stopped struggling. He grabbed at her pants as another man said, "hurry up, man, I want my turn!" He moved towards the two.

Abel dropped down quickly next to the girl. The man that had been moving towards them stopped suddenly, falling sideways from his unsteady gait. Abel looked down and saw that the girl was breathing but unconscious. Her face was bloody and bruised. He glanced around him at the startled men and saw the figure that had been lying to the side begin to moan and stir. A full five seconds passed as Abel took a deep breath and counted, purposely slowing his reaction.

Abel sprung at the man who was on top of the girl. The impact of his open-handed slap to the man's face broke his jaw. Abel's follow up punch to his gut ruptured his spleen and knocked him into the wall behind him with enough force to rupture two disks in his back. Like a blur, Abel moved from man to man and back again, punching and kicking, breaking teeth and bone until he came to the man who had fallen when he dropped off the roof.

The man was wide eyed and pulled a large revolver from his coat as Abel approached. Abel was breathing deeply, calming himself as he walked slowly towards the man, who screamed obscenities and warnings to stop. He fired four shots at Abel, centered on his chest, and then threw the gun as Abel picked him up. Still cussing at Abel loudly, his body sailed through the air and impacted a thick storefront window nearly fifty feet away, just outside the alley.

A loud alarm sounded from the store with the broken window. Abel checked the girl and saw she was breathing, but still unconscious. He moved to the downed figure and saw it was a man. His eyes were clamped shut and he rolled slightly, holding his stomach. Abel saw bullet holes in his left side and his shoulder, but not much blood. He was in no danger of bleeding to death anytime soon.

Abel was weighing whether or not he should carry them both to the hospital when sirens began to wail a few blocks away. Abel leaped to the top of the one-story building, then up to the third-story unit next door. Seconds later a police car pulled up at the store. The two policemen got out and looked inside the window just as some of the battered and broken men in the alley began to wake up and cry out. Minutes later, two more cars pulled up, followed by several ambulances. Abel continued to watch as the EMT's loaded the man and the still unconscious girl into the ambulance. He decided he had enough excitement for the night and turned towards the parking garage.

A few rooftops over he heard a gunshot. He couldn't tell which direction it had come from, so he stopped to listen. Another shot rang out, this time south of him. *Maybe half a mile away,* he thought. Abel moved swiftly in that direction, listening for any type of commotion. He couldn't hear anything out of the ordinary and searched the ground as he leaned over the edge of the roof. Below, what appeared to be a very drunk man fired shots randomly into the sky.

Abel looked around and saw no one. He dropped down over the edge and landed in front of the guy. Only slightly startled, he raised the gun up, intending to point it in Abel's face. Abel quickly took the gun away, broke it in two, and then handed them back to the man. He protested in an unintelligible language, and took a swing at Abel. Something inside the man's clenched fist cracked loudly as it struck Abel's jaw. He grabbed his hand and cradled it, screaming loudly in pain. He sat down hard, weeping.

Abel heard a scream come from above him. He looked up, scanning the tall building across the street. It was an old hotel used mostly by transients and the semi-homeless. He heard the scream again and saw a broken window four stories up. There was a fire escape that ran near it. He leapt to the fourth floor fire escape and jumped over to the window, which had a small ledge. Inside, he saw a woman cradling a small, bloody bundle.

He broke through the rest of the window and entered quickly. The lady screamed, but continued to hold the bundle.

"It's okay, I'm a good guy! What happened?" Abel shouted.

The women held the bundle tight. She shakily replied, "my baby was shot! We were looking out the window and she got shot!"

Abel quickly realized the bundle wasn't crying and his blood ran cold and he said, "please, let me take a look!"

She handed the baby gently to Abel, who opened the blood-soaked blanket. The baby's eyes were opened weakly and he saw the bullet had nearly taken off the baby's upper right arm. He ripped the edge of the blanket off and tied a tourniquet around the top of the arm, above the wound.

He turned to the lady and shouted, "I'll get her to the hospital!" Abel didn't wait for a reply. There were two hospitals within a few miles. The county hospital was closest so he leapt in that direction. Running full out, leaping from rooftop to rooftop, even skipping over entire buildings, Abel realized he needed to get to the ground so he could run faster.

He hit the ground in the middle of Chester Ave. Without slowing, he ran down the middle of the street, dodging cars as needed. He leapt over a busy intersection and landed on top of a car waiting to turn, leaving a large dent as he continued on, and hitting the doorway of the ER a few seconds later. Luckily the doors had been opened as he likely would have broken through trying to slow down.

"I need help!" he yelled as he came to a stop in the quiet ER. Looking around at stunned faces, he moved towards the nurses' station, knocking two latched doors off their hinges. Two nurses, seeing the blood-soaked blanket moved towards Abel quickly.

"Freeze!" screamed a security guard, a pistol drawn and pointed at Abel. The nurses stopped abruptly, their senses overriding their training.

Abel realized he still had his mask on. He said quickly but calmly, "I have a baby with a gunshot wound to her arm. I put a tourniquet on less than two minutes ago. She needs help now!" He moved to hand the baby to the nurses, who accepted her gently and immediately laid her on a gurney and began triage. A doctor ran into the room also and they quickly moved the patient into another area to continue working.

The security guard kept his pistol pointed at Abel. "You need to take that mask off, mister!" he exclaimed.

"I can't do that, sir," Abel replied. He turned slowly towards the door.

"If you move, I will shoot!" the guard shouted, obviously shaken by what had happened.

A voice came from the waiting room. "He just saved a baby, man, let him go!"

"How do I know he didn't shoot her in the first place?" the guard shouted.

"I'm walking out that door, sir. If you shoot, you won't hurt me, but you might hurt someone else." Abel moved closer to the door.

"Let him go, man," someone yelled from the small crowd of people that had started filling in the room.

Abel suddenly sprinted out the door, gone too fast for the guard to respond. He jumped up to the two-story building across the parking lot and was soon several blocks away. He moved quickly along the rooftops until he was across from the parking garage. His wallet and keys were right where he left them. He checked for people and seeing none, hopped over to the third story. He bent down and weaved through the parked cars, getting to his truck. He unlocked the door and got in slowly, taking off his mask and gloves. There he sat for a few minutes, listening to his heart beat.

After a few minutes, he slowly pulled out of the garage and made his way to I-99. He drove home on the sparse interstate. He exited and drove through a very quiet Shafter and then on home. He was driving on automatic pilot and though it took forty-five minutes to get home, he didn't remember the drive at all. He was preoccupied with a night of blood and violence.

As he pulled into the driveway, he could see there were no lights on. Andy had obviously gone to bed already. He unlocked the door and walked in. It was almost 11:30pm, but he decided to check the news to see if there was any mention of what had happened. He left the lights out and turned the TV on, keeping the volume low. He found one of the local news channels still reviewing the sports news of the day. He sat back on the couch and rubbed his eyes as they went to commercial. His other hand fell on his chest where he discovered four bullet holes in his shirt and a lot of blood that wasn't his.

When the news came back on, the anchor had a strange look on his face. Reading from a sheet of paper instead of the teleprompter, he stumbled over his words slightly:

Breaking news this hour. This is a developing story so we caution that a lot of this information is evolving. There was a lot of activity downtown this Saint Patrick's evening as a...masked man...burst into the county hospital ER carrying a...baby...suffering from a gunshot wound. According to eyewitness reports, the man...dressed in...completely in black...ran through the door carrying the wounded infant, broke the solid wood doors leading to the triage area and handed the child off to emergency personnel. When a security guard tried to stop him, he...ran away at a very high rate of speed and... This is according to several eyewitnesses...leaped up to the top of a two-story building. As incredible as this sounds...we are currently queuing up some cell phone video of the event as I speak...we have it?...Is it ready? Okay, this is unedited so we apologized for anything that might offend viewers.

Abel watched with astonishment as the entire scene replayed on TV. A girl was being recorded by her friend as she waited to get her arm bandaged. The camera panned over as Abel had kicked the doors off their hinges, the doors nearly hitting someone waiting in a wheelchair. He looked like an insane person, masked, yelling, covered in blood and then running away. *Andy is not going to be happy*, he thought.

The anchor continued:

More information is coming in. Earlier in the evening, also downtown, a masked man…presumably the same man…intervened and stopped a gang rape of a young woman. Now all of this is alleged, but it appears the young woman and her boyfriend were attacked and dragged in an alley where the boyfriend was shot and is in critical condition. The girl was apparently beaten and nearly sexually assaulted and at some point the…masked man… intervened. Four of the six men are in serious condition and two are in critical condition…multiple broken bones, bruised organs, head trauma…

The anchor was handed another paper, which he scanned. Then he continued:

Apparently, the mother of the baby has been found. She showed up at the hospital a few minutes after the masked man. According to the mother…she heard gunshots from her apartment and walked to the window to see what was going on…carrying her child. She saw a man on the ground shooting into the sky and…again this is the mother…when he saw her, he shot at her, hitting the baby. A few minutes later, the masked man burst through the window and took the baby. She ran to the window and saw him…jumping across the rooftops…running faster than she could believe, and jumping thirty to forty feet at a time. The baby is expected to survive. We will have more information on this breaking story on our morning newscast tomorrow.

The anchors exchanged words of disbelief and gratefulness to the masked man, but Abel didn't hear any of it. He wept bitterly, his sobs loud enough to wake Andrea. She hurried into the living room, seeing Abel, his head in his hands, shuddering as he cried. She ran to him and held him tight as he buried his face in her shoulder.

Chapter 11

Two Weeks Later

Video of the masked man had been picked up on multiple cameras, including several inside and outside the hospital, traffic cameras, and even store cameras. Astonishingly, the store which Abel threw the shooter through had a camera trained right on the alley. Decent video had been recorded not only of what happened in the alley, but also showing the man flying at and through the window. It was all over the internet. Abel's parkour-like run above and down Chester Ave was largely recorded and pieced together from multiple vantage points along the road. Businesses in the area poured over their recorded camera footage from that night and every other night they had available looking for shots of the masked man.

Tom had been at the forefront of a lot of the information. Andrea had called him that night and he rushed to the paper to find a flurry of activity. It had hardly died down a bit in the ensuing weeks. His editor wanted him to write about the local reaction to the masked man so he wrote a nice fluff piece on the importance of heroes. Of course, a few people pointed out his own possible brush with the masked man during his suicide attempt, but Tom laughed it off and it was largely ignored.

Following a long call into a local radio station's afternoon program, even Pete Zisk had gotten some attention. He claimed to have been studying the masked man for years and even got the press to start using the moniker 'The Angel.' He had become a regular on a few local radio programs and had appeared on several cable news shows over the last week.

Recently Pete had updated his page for The Angel and included an interesting run-in with hunters in the Sierras who were beaten and had their rifles taken, bent and thrown in a tree. He added several other local run-ins in Kern County where people had been saved or stopped from doing something stupid. He was getting a lot of web traffic which was leading to a lot of ad revenue. Pete promised many more updates in the coming weeks.

Tom had tried to see Abel and Andrea a few times, but Andrea kept telling him not to. Abel didn't want to see anyone right now. He had even skipped their church services for the last few Sundays and Wednesdays. He was obviously very depressed and worried about what might happen.

Tom finally decided it was time to visit, whether Abel wanted him to or not. He drove out to the farm around lunch time. It was quiet. Tom parked and walked up to the door. Andrea opened it before he could knock. They embraced and it lasted a full minute.

"Where is he?" Tom asked.

"Out at the barn," Andrea replied. "He's out there all day. Working on equipment or just sitting and staring off. Won't even come in for lunch. I've been taking it to him." She stared out at the barn as she spoke. "Tom, I've never seen him like this. He is always so upbeat, even when he's sad he puts on a happy face. Its…weird."

"I'll go out and talk to him," Tom said, walking off towards the barn. As he got closer, he heard the sound of machinery being worked on. He opened the door and saw Abel, sticking out from underneath a tractor.

"Is it lunch time already, Andy?" he asked not looking out.

"Soon," Tom replied. "I wanted to talk with you first."

Tom heard an audible sigh as Abel paused what he was doing. He began to roll out and said, "I told you I was fine, Tom." He stood up, wiping his hands on a rag.

"You're not fine, Abel. You've been through a terrible trauma. Nobody expects you to be fine. Even people trained to deal with it would have trouble coping with what you experienced." Tom intoned the words with as much compassion as he had mixed with a tinge of anger.

"I'm not traumatized," Abel insisted, incredulously. He walked over to the table and sat down.

Tom followed. "Then what is going on, Abel?"

"I feel bad. Bad for what I did."

"You saved at least three lives, Abel. Why would you feel bad?" Tom suspected why, but he thought it might be good for Abel to say it aloud.

"Because I was sloppy and arrogant and didn't think of the consequences. There were probably twenty different ways I could have saved the baby without getting on camera. And the jerks in the alley, I could have killed them. I was stupid to think I should be doing the job of the police. They've been trained. I'm just a strong idiot looking for a thrill. And now I may have exposed my secret and destroyed my life and Andy's. I can't even look at her."

Tom laughed a little and Abel gave him an angry look. "Sorry Abel, I'm not laughing at you. The baby, Leslie is her name by the way, the doctors say the tourniquet helped, but just a few more minutes would have meant her life. The ambulance wouldn't have gotten there in time. And any way you got her there would have put you on camera.

Sure, it was a dramatic entrance, but not entirely unnecessary. It sure got their attention, didn't it?"

"I suppose," Abel conceded. "But I almost hit someone with the door. And if that guard had shot, he had no way of knowing it would ricochet. I could have killed someone."

"Maybe or maybe not. It didn't happen, though. And as far as me or Andrea or anyone else is concerned, the punks in the alley got what they deserved. They're still alive, but they will never forget the lesson you taught them."

"I was mad. I could have stopped them without hurting them so badly. I'm not a judge, heck I'm not even a cop. I could have yelled and they probably would have stopped. I could have just stopped the one guy hurting the girl, but I let my anger get the better of me." Abel's eyes drew downward. "I'm no better than them. They let their lusts get the better of them, I let my anger." Abel stopped talking for a moment and then continued, "you know, I haven't even prayed about it? I haven't asked God to forgive me. I don't think I deserve it."

Tom wasn't much for prayers, though he had done his share in his life. He knew Abel, however, prayed many times throughout the day. For him to miss a day, much less a few weeks, was very uncharacteristic.

"Abel, I'm not a praying man, at least not a good one," Tom said. "But I do know from what little exposure I have had to the Bible that praying is the first thing Christians are supposed to do when they have a problem. Isn't forgiveness kind of a guarantee if you ask for it?"

"If you are sincerely asking for it, then yeah, the Lord forgives just about anything. But I'm ashamed to even ask for it."

"You're human, Abel, despite your abilities. You make mistakes. You are obviously feeling the sting of what you have done and want forgiveness. It's not like God doesn't know what you did."

Abel looked thoughtfully away for a moment, then back at Tom. "You're right. I put it off for too long." Abel began to bow his head.

"Well, I'm going to check on lunch. I haven't had Andrea's cooking in weeks and I'm going through withdrawals." Tom said this while walking towards the door. "Come inside when you're done and we can eat together." Tom still wasn't comfortable with 'group prayer' as he called it, but he knew Abel and Andrea were. Abel looked up at him and smiled, shaking his head a little as he bowed.

Tom walked into the kitchen through the back door. It smelled incredible! *I don't know what Andrea is making*, he thought, *but I'd eat a shoe if it smelled like that.*

Andrea was putting the dishes out on the table and Tom offered to take over. They chatted like good friends who hadn't seen each other in a while. He enjoyed helping her in the kitchen, at least what help he could be. A few minutes later Abel came in the back door, his red eyes showing recent tears and a big grin on his face.

"Well, you look better," Andrea commented.

"I feel better," Abel replied.

The three friends sat down at the table. Abel removed his hat and said Grace and they began to eat. Fried chicken, mashed potatoes and green beans with a healthy Mason jar of sweet tea. Tom ate slowly, savoring every bite.

As they finished the meal, Abel began to speak, "thanks to both of you for putting up with me." He smiled and took Andrea's hand. "I won't be doing that any more Andy. I put us both in a lot of jeopardy and it won't happen again. I'm sorry."

Andrea smiled. "I know what helping people means to you, Abel. I don't want you to stop. Maybe the whole 'looking-for-trouble' thing could stop, but I think you should carry the mask and gloves with you in your truck. You never know when you might need them." She put her other hand on top of their clasped hands.

"Yeah, okay, I can do that," Abel insisted. "But no more patrolling. It was just a matter of time before something happened that I wasn't prepared for. Low key, that's my new way of doing things."

Tom laughed. "With all this free time, maybe you should get a girlfriend?" He laughed again.

Neither Andrea nor Abel laughed. They each looked at each other with a half-smile, which was fading. Tom noticed the discomfort and remembered his conversation with Andrea the day Abel attacked the hunters.

"I said something wrong, didn't I?" Tom asked.

"It's okay, Tom," Abel teased with a wry smile. "I decided a long time ago that I would not subject a woman to my life. My secrets are a lot to bear."

"So, you won't date at all?" Tom asked.

"I don't even allow myself in a room alone with a woman, other than Andy. Keeps temptation at bay. Learned that one from Billy Graham."

"Don't you get, you know, lonely?"

"Don't you?" Abel asked.

Tom thought for a minute. He had been lonely until he met Andrea and Abel. Now he wasn't. He hadn't actually been intimate with anyone in a long time, since he was still married, and oddly enough he didn't really miss it that much. He guessed the longer a person went, the less it mattered. Of course, he was looking forward to resuming that activity someday. Still, the idea of Abel never experiencing the emotional attachment that a couple has saddened him.

"Have you ever been in love?" Tom asked.

Both Andrea and Abel looked at each other. "Once, a long time ago," Abel replied. "When I was 14. Her name was Sylvia. I really liked her and I think the feeling was mutual."

Andrea chimed in, "You 'think' the feeling was mutual? She practically threw herself at you for months," she recounted. She looked towards Tom. "As much as a 14-year old girl can, anyway."

"What happened," Tom asked.

"She had a heart defect no one knew about. We were all on a youth retreat hiking up near Mammoth. I was a mile or so up the trail, showing off with the rest of the boys. The girls were headed up a steep hill and she just fell over. The youth minister tried giving her CPR, but it was too late. Andy was there. She saw it happen. Probably was a good thing I wasn't there. I might have picked her up and tried to run her to a hospital." Abel gave a quiet laugh as he said the last words. "I haven't gotten close to another girl since. It's not just that I'm afraid of loss, but after what happened to my mom…" Abel railed off. "Well, I just couldn't run the risk."

"You don't have to get your wife pregnant, you know. There are ways to prevent it," Tom declared.

"I know, but it's weird way to start a conversation 'Hi I'm Abel Hodges. You aren't by chance infertile, are you?'"

They all laughed heartily. Andrea added, "there are several single women at our church that have had their tubes tied. They are a little older than Abel, though. I've tried playing matchmaker."

"Yeah, but I wouldn't want someone with *me* only because it was convenient. Those ladies, nice as they are, just don't click with me. I want a love like dad talked about with mom. They deserve the whole package and so do I. At least if I ever was going to let it happen." Abel's words rang true in their ears and both Tom and Andrea agreed. Tom was pretty sure Andrea had snuck a few sideways glances at him during Abel's reply. He looked at her and smiled.

They sat unspeaking for a few minutes as they finished their iced tea, then Abel spoke again. "Well, I've got work to finish up in the shop." He rose and grabbed his hat. "Thanks for lunch, Andy. Tom, I'll see you later." He started to walk towards the door and stopped. "You guys want to go up to the mountains this weekend? I skipped last week and I'm gettin' sore." He rubbed his arms and shoulders as he spoke.

"I'm up for it," Tom replied.

"Cool, you guys can make the plans. See you then."

"See ya, Abel," Tom said as Abel closed the door.

Tom turned to Andrea. "So, I'll be here about 7?" he asked.

"Seven is good," she replied with a thoughtful look on her face. Then she asked, "what are we, Tom?"

Chapter 12

"Pardon?" Tom asked.

"Are we just friends, are we a couple? I can't tell," Andrea declared.

Tom was caught off guard. "I don't really know, Andrea. I feel like we're all three friends, but I feel something between us. I don't know what it is, but I feel completely at ease around you. I'm happier when I am with you. I miss you when I'm not with you."

Andrea smiled. "See, that is what I'm feeling. We've both been married before. I never felt like this with Rex. I don't know if that's a good thing or not. I like you, a lot."

"I like you too, Andrea. I don't if it's love or not, but I really like you and I like spending time with you. I feel like we're a couple…" Tom trailed off.

"Me too," Andrea said. "Don't get me wrong, I'm not trying to hurry things up. I just feel like we've gotten to the point where we need to label our relationship. Does that sound weird?"

"Not at all. My dad has been asking to meet you for some time and I keep putting it off, not really knowing where we stand."

"I would love to meet him," she stated.

"Good, I'll set it up, then." Tom stood from his chair and leaned toward her, kissing her on the cheek. "I'm glad we got that settled."

Andrea stood and they hugged. Tom then began to move towards the front door. Andrea followed. As he opened it, he turned and said, "I'll call you later about Saturday." As he did, Andrea grabbed his face and kissed him deeply on the mouth. At first, he was startled, but slowly settled into it, embracing her. Abel, who was standing near the shop entrance smiled widely then turned and went through the door.

When they parted, they just smiled at each other. Tom left the house and got into his car, still smiling. He drove down the dirt road, passed Homer's nearly rebuilt home. He pulled out on the main road and drove towards Shafter. At the first stop light, he habitually glanced in the rearview mirror and saw several cars behind him slowing as they came to the light. He looked forward again and drove on when the light changed.

After a few blocks, it suddenly dawned on him that one of the cars behind him looked familiar and he glanced again. Two cars behind was a dusty El Camino similar to the one he had seen the day Pete Zisk approached him at the coffee shop. He had assumed the car belonged to Zisk since it was the only one in the lot that morning. *Was Zisk following him again*, he thought.

He kept driving until he was nearly home, the El Camino still several cars behind him the whole way. He decided to turn into the same coffee shop he met Zisk at and see if the car followed. As he turned into the lot and found a parking spot, the dusty El Camino pulled in and stopped on the opposite side of the lot. Tom stared at the car, trying to see anything through the dusty windows. If it was Pete Zisk in the car, he couldn't tell.

He waited, but no one got out. After a few minutes, Tom got tired of waiting. He walked very quickly towards the car as the door opened. Pete Zisk got out and stood up just as Tom landed a haymaker to the side of his jaw. Zisk went down; sliding against the car, but Tom picked him up, slamming his back against the car door. He was bigger and heavier, but Tom was livid.

"Why the heck are you following me?" Tom exclaimed. He was angrier than he could ever remember.

"Take it easy, man," Zisk sloppily yelled back. He was trying to break Tom's grasp, but between Tom's intense anger and the blow to his head, he wasn't having much luck. Tom went to hit him again, but Zisk cowered enough that Tom stopped.

"Answer me! Why were you following me?" He let Zisk go, but didn't back away.

"Alright, man, alright," he replied sheepishly. "Let's go inside and I'll explain everything."

"Explain it now!"

"No way, man, you're too mad and I don't feel like getting hit again. At least inside you'll have to behave or they'll call the cops." Zisk put his hands down to his side.

"How about I just keep beating on you until you talk?" Tom spat.

"The first punch is free," Zisk said, picking up his shirt to reveal a pistol-sized Taser, "but the next one will cost you. If you want to talk, go inside and wait for me. If not, I'm out of here."

Tom began to calm down. "Fine, let's go inside." Tom turned around and walked towards the door. He went inside and ordered a cup of coffee, then sat in the back. A few minutes later, Pete Zisk walked in. He ordered what looked like a large milkshake, and then sat down across from Tom. He sat his large tablet on the table. Tom glared at him.

"I know about Abel Hodges," Zisk declared. Tom's stare became more intense.

"Who?" Tom deflected.

"Yeah, that glare in your eyes says you know who I'm talking about. If you get any ideas, my Taser is currently pointed straight at your balls." Tom's stare relaxed a bit.

"Abel Hodges is an organic farmer I've been interviewing for an article. What about him?"

"Cut the crap, Tom. I've been aware of Abel Hodges for months. He's the Angel."

Tom laughed out loud. "Really, got a picture with his wings? Maybe his little harp?" Tom continued laughing.

"Last year after your suicide attempt you accessed my website looking for information on the Angel. I have the MAC address of your lap top from prior conversations."

Tom interrupted, "What's a Mac address? I don't even own a Mac." He said it still half laughing.

"A MAC address is a unique IP number given to your network card when it is manufactured. Put simply, it is a permanent identification for your computer and only your computer. It's what the FBI uses to catch online pedophiles. I recorded yours a few years ago and programmed my server software to tell me if you ever visited my website. It's actually very easy to do."

Tom didn't understand much of what Zisk was saying. "You bugged my computer?"

"No, I bugged mine. In order for one computer to talk to another, you have to give your MAC address. It's like caller ID. Oh, sophisticated hackers can use fake ones, but most people are as uneducated about the internet as you." Zisk was being smug, obviously very proud of himself. "Once you visited, I could see exactly what you were looking at. My 'Angel Page.' I could tell what you were doing with the map, moving it and zooming in on the Hodges farm. I even backtracked into your computer and accessed your camera to make sure it was you."

"You what?" Tom felt himself getting mad again.

"Take it easy, man, I only did it once to make sure it was you. Seriously, if I'm one number off it might be a computer from Zambia. I had to make sure. The next morning, I went to Hodges Farms but I saw you turn on the dirt road before me so I kept going. I drove around the backside of one of the orchards, then up through trees and clearly saw you parked at their house. I've had them under surveillance ever since."

"What do you mean under surveillance?"

"Nothing too high-tech. That stuff's expensive. I have a good camera with a good zoom lens. I put a cheap tracker on that old blue truck of his when he was parked at the grocery store. I know you spend a great deal of time with them, especially his sister." Zisk smiled as he spoke the last sentence. "I've placed trail cameras at the place in the mountains he always goes on the weekend. They are across the river, but the pictures are sometimes good enough to see his face."

"What's the point of all this, Zisk? You've been on TV. You could have exposed Abel any time. Why haven't you?"

"I could give you some BS about it not being the right time or I wanted to make sure I had everything in place, you know, solid evidence. But believe it or not, the real reason is you."

"Me? What do I have to do with it?"

"I've seen the way you act around his sister. You two are obviously in love. I know what life has been like for you, man, and I really do consider you a friend. I didn't want to turn your life upside down again. If Abel gets outed as The Angel, their lives are gonna get crazy."

"And now? Have things changed?" Tom asked quizzingly.

"No, nothing has changed in that department. I'm not telling anyone about Abel Hodges. I don't want to and I don't need to. My website has so much traffic now I had to buy more bandwidth. I have local people coming out of the woodwork to tell me their stories. Next week I have a meeting with a cable network for a reality TV show. Frankly, if I gave up Abel Hodges, that would take all the cameras off me and point them at him. Why do you think they haven't actually found Bigfoot yet? It would be bad for the Bigfoot industry."

Tom hadn't thought of it that way. Still, he couldn't trust Zisk. "This…secret," he started, "this secret that you know is not mine to trust you with. You need to speak to Abel and Andrea. You need to tell them what you know. You need to meet them in their home and realize that they are good people just in case you ever decide to destroy their world for some more press."

Zisk got wide-eyed. "I don't think I want him to know about me. I've seen what he can do when he gets angry."

"He's not likely to get that angry. He'll be sad, sure, but he's not a mindless idiot. He can control himself."

"Did you see what he did to those guys in the alley? Most of them had life altering injuries. Two of them may never walk again unassisted. I've seen what happens when he gets mad and I want no part of it." Zisk's hands were shaking as he spoke.

"Tough!" Tom spat as he leaned across the table, getting closer to Zisk's face. "You wanted in on this, you've been doing the cloak and dagger stuff all this time, well, now buddy you get to go *all* in. One way or another, Abel will find out. Trust me; he would respect you a lot more if you told him yourself."

Pete Zisk thought for a moment. "Okay, I'll do it. But I want witnesses. I want you and his sister there. I don't think he'd hurt me in front of her."

"Done," Tom said. "Saturday morning at 7:30, we'll all be at the farm. I won't tell them why you're stopping by, so be ready to tell them everything."

"Okay," Zisk replied sheepishly. Then he chuckled and shook his head. "You know what's really funny about this, Tom?"

"What's that?"

"This was going to be the last time I went out there. I was done after today. You would have never known anything about this if I didn't choose to go out there one more time. And I don't even know why I went. The idea just came to me and I decided to go. Man, if I believed in God, I'd swear He had something to do with it."

"Don't swear to God," Tom said getting up from his seat. "It's blasphemy."

Chapter 13

Saturday morning, Tom, Abel and Andrea were finishing breakfast and getting their things together for the drive up the mountain. Tom kept looking at his watch and out the window. Andrea finally noticed and asked playfully, "Are you expecting a cab, Mister?"

Tom, realizing what he was doing, laughingly said, "No, just wondering if it's chilly up there."

"Maybe a little. Best to bring a jacket this time of year anyway. You never know if it will snow or rain or whatever," Andrea explained.

"Yeah, you're right," Tom agreed. It was nearly 8AM and Pete Zisk was nowhere to be found. They would be leaving in a few minutes. If Pete didn't get there soon, Tom was going to have to let them in on it. They continued getting ready, but by 8:15 Tom was ready to spill the beans.

"Could you guys come in here?" Tom asked from the kitchen.

Both Abel and Andrea walked in and saw Tom sitting at the kitchen table. He had a very serious look on his face. "Why don't you guys have a seat? I have something important to tell you." He motioned to the chairs as he spoke.

"Well, you sound serious," Andrea observed through a smile as she took a seat.

Both sat and Tom began, "Yesterday when I left, I noticed someone following me. I thought I knew who it was so I pulled over at a coffee shop near my house. It turned out to be Pete Zisk."

"Isn't that the guy who you talked to before you figured out who Abel was?" Andrea asked.

"That's the guy," Tom pointed out. "Well, he knows."

"Knows?" Abel asked. "About…me?"

"Unfortunately," Tom said, looking down. "| It's my fault."

"What do you mean, Tom?" Andrea responded, taking his hand.

"I guess he somehow tagged my computer so that he knew when I logged onto his website. He could see what page I was on and how I manipulated the map to see your farm. Then he saw me coming out here and has been surveilling you ever since."

Abel and Andrea looked at each other and sighed. "What does he want?" Abel asked.

"According to him, he doesn't want anything. As long as there is a mystery around 'the Angel,' he is in the spotlight. He's getting publicity and he's making money because of it. He was supposed to come out here this morning and meet with you."

"And he hasn't shown?" Abel asked. "Can you call him?"

"I don't have his number," Tom stated. "But he can't be that hard to find. I do know he was a little scared of you, but I really thought he would show." Tom thought for a minute. "I think I can get his contact info. The paper had a reporter interview him and I bet they have a way to contact him."

Tom got out his phone and made a few calls. It was slow because it was Saturday and there weren't many people in the office, but he finally managed to track down the reporter. A few minutes later he had Pete Zisk's cell phone number and address.

Tom tried his cell phone several times and got no answer. He left a short message for Pete to contact him. "I don't know where he is," Tom said. "He doesn't seem like the kinda guy that goes off the grid."

"Unless he's trying to hide," Abel suggested. "Maybe he got scared and took off. Why don't we just go to his house?"

"Alright," Tom nodded. He looked at the address he had written down. "Looks like he doesn't live very far from me. Shouldn't take too long to get there."

The three loaded up into Abel's truck and headed off. As they passed, Tom looked over at Homer Todd's house. "He's nearly finished," Tom observed. "It's looking good."

"Yeah," Andrea marveled. "It's amazing that he can make it look like it's 100 years old when it's brand new. His grandson is a great carpenter."

"Jem's great with his hands period. I've hired him on a few times when I needed extra help. He's a good kid," Abel added.

The idle chatter continued for the next 20 minutes while they drove to Pete Zisk's house. When they got there, Tom didn't see the old El Camino anywhere. It was an older home, but in good repair and the lawn was neat and tidy. This was not what Tom expected. The three got out and walked up to the door.

An elderly woman opened the door but kept the chain on. "If you're looking for Petey, he ain't here. Should be back in a couple hours," the lady stated.

"My name is Tom Salem, ma'am. We had an appointment and he didn't show. Do you know if he went somewhere else?"

"He didn't say where he was going. He just told me he had an appointment and would be back in a couple of hours. He comes and goes a lot, especially since he started gettin' noticed by the media." She thought for a few seconds before remarking, "All I can tell you is he left about an hour ago. Sorry."

"Thank you, ma'am. Could you let him know I came by if you see him?"

"Yah sir, I will," she replied.

Tom, Abel and Andrea walked back to the car. Once they got in, Abel asked, "So what should we do?"

"I guess we should just head back to your place in case he comes by," Tom said.

They drove back towards the farm. All three were steeped in their own thoughts until they turned onto the dirt road that led to the Hodge's home. There was an ambulance and several sheriffs' vehicles parked at Homer's house. The three got out and approached the house. On the lawn were two bodies covered in yellow blankets.

Andrea gasped and grabbed at Tom. Abel's heart sank and he started to run towards the house, barely remembering to keep it slow. A deputy came out of the house and stopped him on the front porch.

"Sir, this is a crime scene. I'll have to ask you to step back a bit," the deputy instructed, putting his hand out to stop Abel.

"This is my neighbor's house. I've known him all my life. Please, can you tell me what's going on?"

By this time, Tom and Andrea, hands clasped tight, were coming up the front steps. Homer's grandson, Jem, came out the door. His young face was bright red and his eyes puffy from the tears.

"Mr. Hodges?" he asked.

"Yeah, Jem. What happened? Where's Homer?"

Jem sniffed. "He's over on the ground, with that fat ba…." He caught himself before finishing.

A deputy sheriff came out next who Abel knew. "Abel, Andrea," he greeted, tipping his head toward them.

"Carlos, what happened to Homer?" Abel asked.

"We're still trying to piece it together. Homer and Jem were working on the house. Jem says he was upstairs running the table saw so he didn't hear anything until the gunshot. He came down to check it out and the big guy had a hole in his chest and Homer had been hit by a Taser. I guess his heart couldn't take it. By the time we got here with the ambulance, it was too late for either." He turned to the young man. "I'm so sorry, Jem. Homer was one of the finest men I knew."

"Thank you, sir," Jem said. "Can I call my mom and them now?"

"Sure, buddy," Carlos replied. "Are you sure you don't want me to do it?" the officer asked.

"Nah, sir. I'll do it," the boy said.

With that Jem began walking off the porch, taking out his cell phone and dialing. He disappeared around the side of the house.

Carlos looked at Abel, Tom and Andrea. "I know Homer carried a 1911. He has since the 50's. I'm guessing that's a .45 hole in the big guy's chest. Most likely Homer had the gun drawn and the big guy fired the Taser at him. Not the smartest thing to do when someone has their finger on the trigger. I don't know why Homer would have drawn his gun, though."

105

Tom spoke up first. "The bug guy's name is Pete Zisk. He's a website operator dealing with paranormal stuff in Kern County."

The deputy looked directly into Tom's eyes. "And you are?"

"My name is Tom Salem. I write for the Bakersfieldian. Pete contacted me from time to time when I had articles that touched on his line of work. He did a story on Homer awhile back."

"I thought he looked familiar. I've seen his website. He's part of this 'Angel' business, isn't he?"

"Yeah, he was probably trying to link the 'Angel' to what happened to Homer when his house burned down. He was supposed to meet us this morning at Abel's house. He had some questions about what happened at Homer's house the night of the fire and Abel had been the one to find Homer on the lawn. We've been trying to reach him on his phone. We just got back from his house. I don't know why he was here, though." Tom knew he was lying but he didn't know what else to say. He really had no idea why Pete Zisk would be at Homer's house or why Homer would pull a gun on him. He glanced at Abel and they each nodded slightly.

"I already recovered his cell phone and its battery is dead. That's probably why you couldn't reach him. Maybe when he finally got to Abel's place and you weren't there he came by here to see if Homer knew where you were," Carlos mused. "Homer would have seen if you guys left since this is the main road out of here." He walked over to the dusty El Camino and peered into the bed. "Well, there's a tire and a jack in the bed. He probably had a flat on the way to see you."

Carlos stroked his chin as he pondered. "Homer liked everyone, but he had little patience for people he didn't know. A few years ago, I got called out here because he pulled his gun on a Census worker. Homer probably didn't want to talk to him and the big guy wouldn't

106

take no for an answer, so Homer pulled his gun to scare him off. The big guy fired the Taser and the gun went off. Big guy was killed by the gun shot; Homer was hit by the Taser and probably suffered a heart attack." Carlos shook his head and threw up his arms. "That's my working theory anyway. We'll do an investigation, of course, but I'm sure we'll find something like this." The deputy began to rub his temples. "What a mess."

Andrea spoke next, "I'm going to check on Jem." She walked around the building to find him.

"There's the coroner," Carlos said pointing to the end of the drive. "If you'll excuse me…" He moved toward the approaching van.

"Thanks, Carlos," Abel said as the deputy walked away. Abel and Tom walked towards Abel's truck to get out of the way of the coroner. Both men were silent as they tried to process the events of the morning.

Chapter 14

By summer the investigation was over. The Sheriff's office and County Coroner's official findings mirrored that of Deputy Carlos'. It was an accidental shooting caused by the discharge of the Taser. While no one could know exactly what led up to the confrontation, the outcome and fault had been determined and the case was closed.

Jem had graduated high school was already living in Homer's house. Homer had fortunately deeded the house and small acreage to him a few months prior to his death. Abel had hired Jem to work with him at Hodges Farms. Even Tom was spending more time working at the farm when time allowed. He found it very satisfying working with his hands and wrote about it often.

On the one-year anniversary of his suicide attempt, Tom asked Andrea to marry him. They were walking through her garden after dinner, flowers in full bloom, when he bent down on one knee and popped the question. Since their father was deceased, Tom had asked Abel his opinion and he was ecstatic. Andrea gave an emphatic, "yes!" and they sealed it with a kiss. They planned on a spring wedding.

At the beginning of November, Andrea and Tom arrived home one Wednesday afternoon after the Farmers Market to find Abel gone. His truck was there as were the various farm vehicles. Andrea called his cell phone to see if he was going to be home for dinner but got no answer. After a few hours, Tom called Jem to see if Abel was there and he said he hadn't seen him all day.

Andrea was worried. It wasn't like Abel to be out of touch for so long. And why were his vehicles there? Even if he had been on foot, he would answer his phone. Andrea went to bed and Tom slept on the couch, waiting to hear from Abel.

The next morning, Andrea was on the phone with the Sheriff's department letting them know Abel was missing. While they couldn't open anything official since Abel was an adult and no foul play was expected, the office was small enough that everyone that patrolled the area was keeping an eye out for him. Tom walked around the property looking for any clues about Abel's whereabouts. He could find nothing to explain his disappearance.

As Tom walked back to the house, he passed through the garden. A lot of the flowers had lost their blooms as the days shortened, but it was still beautiful. He walked along the stone pathway, admiring the plants on either side when he caught the scent of fresh dirt. He walked around a bit more until he found an area where the dirt had been recently disturbed. It smelled very strongly of fresh soil, but it was neat and tidy.

The idea flashed through his mind that someone had killed Abel and buried his body here. Tom actually chuckled at the idea. Who could kill Abel? And how could they do it without making a heck of a mess. Still, he filed the disturbed soil in his memory.

Tom came in through the kitchen door and found Andrea weeping gently on the couch. He sat next to his fiancé on the couch and held her as she cried.

That night, Tom and Andrea watched the late news together. Tom had planned to stay with Andrea for a while. He would use the couch as it seemed weird to use Abel's bed. Just as they were both beginning to nod off on the couch a report made both of them perk up.

News tonight of a possible plane crash in the high Sierras. Backpackers returning from a back-country snowshoeing trip near Overlook Mountain say they observed a small, white plane fall out of the sky several miles away from them yesterday afternoon. When they attempted to reach the crash site, they were forced to turn back as the terrain became too treacherous and a severe storm was approaching. Rescuers have not been able to search the area from the sky or ground due to the strong early winter snow storm. The search is expected to pick up tomorrow morning when better weather has been forecasted. So far, no local airports have reported any aircraft as overdue or missing.

Tom and Andrea looked at each other, eyes wide. They both quickly got up and ran outside towards the back of the barn. Abel's old Cessna was gone. Tom hadn't noticed earlier as the rusting aircraft had always just been part of the backdrop. Andrea began to cry again.

"It was him, wasn't it?" she whispered through tears.

"Too much of a coincidence. But would he survive a plane crash?" Tom wondered aloud.

"I don't know, but if anyone could it would be him." They went back into the house and Andrea called the Sheriff's office to let them know what they found. She was told there was nothing they could do tonight, but they would relay the information to the Tulare County Sheriff in the morning. As soon as Andrea got off the phone with the Sheriff, she immediately began calling members of their congregation asking for prayers for Abel. It was a long, teary night for Andrea and Tom.

The next morning, Tom and Andrea drove to the Tulare County Sheriff's office with pictures of Abel and the Cessna. They knew they could just email or fax them, but they wanted to be closer to the search. The area was too remote to reach my vehicle and covered in too much fresh snow to reach by foot. The helicopter spotted the wreckage and was able to land nearby. They recovered a few items and returned to the airfield. Within an hour, the Sheriff approached Tom and Andrea, who were waiting in his office.

"Well, it was definitely your plane. The markings match perfectly. I'm very sorry, but we did find some remains."

Andrea's eyes widened and then clamped shut as she began to weep. Tom pulled her in close and through tears asked the Sheriff, "Can you tell us anything, yet? Could you tell why it went down?" Tom's voice cracked as he spoke.

"Some major malfunction, I'm sure. The hikers said it was already on fire as it fell. I'm told the wreckage was extremely melted in some places. The remains are badly burned. I don't know if we'll get any DNA off them, but it sounds like we won't need to." The Sheriff's voice was a practiced, but caring tone. Tom appreciated it. "We'll be flying back out there this afternoon to recover what we can. It's very remote, so the wreckage will probably just be left there …unless you want it removed."

"Thank you, Sheriff. We'll let you know. Unless you need anything else, I'd like to take Andrea home."

"Sure, I've got your numbers. We'll be in touch as soon as we've secured the remains."

Tom nodded and led Andrea out of the office. They got into his car and held each other close for a few minutes, then began the long drive home. After a half hour or so, Andrea spoke, "Why would he be flying? And why up there? It makes no sense!"

"I just don't know, Andrea," Tom admitted. "He had said he wanted to complete his pilots' license, but he hadn't spoken of it in months." They continued home in silence, hands clasped together.

112

The next month passed slowly. The Tulare County Sheriff had informed them that they had sifted through the wreckage and recovered the human remains as well as a few personal items. While the remains were too badly burned to identify completely, they could confirm it was a male, likely in his mid to late 20's and over six feet tall. They also found Abel's charred driver's license. The NTSB took over investigation of the crash to determine what happened, but the Sheriff was convinced the remains were indeed those of Abel Hodges and officially declared him killed in the crash. The remains were eventually released to Andrea and she arranged for the funeral.

Tom had taken time off from work to be there for Andrea and to get the farm in order. Jem took on a lot more responsibility, but knew the work well having been raised doing it. While Abel had officially owned the farm, his very short Will had left it for Andrea as well as a $200,000 life insurance policy. Andrea had at first questioned why he had a life insurance policy given the odds of him dying, but in time realized that it was just how Abel was.

A week after Abel's funeral, the NTSB ruled the crash an accident caused by a cracked fuel line. The wreckage was left at the site due to its remote location. The case was officially closed.

Nearly two months after the crash, Andrea decided it was time to pack up Abel's room. She and Tom would be marrying soon and the space was needed for Tom's things. Besides, she thought it might help the healing process. She asked Tom to help her pack up the room, which she hadn't been in since the accident.

Tom and Andrea went into Abel's room. It was dusty, but otherwise immaculate. The bed was made, his usually cluttered desk was neat and tidy and even his closet was perfectly organized.

"It's funny," Andrea remarked. "This is the cleanest I've ever seen his room."

"Really?" Tom Asked. "His shop is so organized I assumed that was just his nature." Tom began folding clothes and putting them in a box.

"That was dad's doin'. He was very organized and demanded it in his shop. Abel was naturally a slob." Andrea laughed as she remembered her brother. "He would misplace stuff all the time. I don't think he ever made his bed."

Tom thought it was odd that the room would be so tidy. *Did Abel somehow know he wasn't coming back,* he thought. Suicide had been ruled out early on since Abel was so devoutly against it. And he had no reason to anyway. Tom also noticed that Abel's 'exercise outfit' was not in the closet, nor was his Kevlar mask. They had already cleaned out his truck and they weren't in there, either. Tom was getting suspicious, but said nothing.

"There are pictures missing," Andrea mused with a quizzical look on her face. "He had a picture of mom and dad and another one of the two of us when we were young. They're usually sitting on the desk." They both looked around the desk and behind it. "Maybe he moved them. I'm sure they'll turn up somewhere."

They continued to pack up his room until there was nothing left. The clothes would be donated. The bed would stay. The TV would stay on the wall and the small radio would stay on the desk near the lamp. Tom thought to himself, *how can a man's whole life fit in a couple of boxes?* He reminded himself it was just a year ago he had packed all of his life into a few boxes, too.

The nagging feeling that something wasn't right stuck with Tom even through the next day. Jem was showing Tom some welding techniques.

"Mr. Salem, you are getting really good at this. No one would ever guess you grew up in the city."

"Thanks, Jem. But most people probably wouldn't call Bakersfield a 'city.' A large town, maybe," Tom replied. "Did your grandpa show you how to weld?"

"A little, some I learned in school. But Abel was my best teacher. He taught me how to weld in the worst conditions, when things aren't working right. Like when it is raining hard or muddy or even when it 110 degrees outside. They don't teach that in school."

"You guys got really close in the last year, huh?"

"Yes sir, he was a great boss. A great friend. Family, really. I'd do just about anything for him," Jem stated. Tom could sense for weeks there was something Jem wanted to say. The closer they got, the more he could feel it. Jem was hiding something. Tom decided now was the time to get it out there.

"Let's take a break. I think there are some cold sodas in the mini-fridge."

They walked over to the fridge and each got a soda. They sat at the kitchenette, setting their welding masks on the table.

"Do you mind if I ask you a question about the day your grandpa died?" Tom asked.

"Sure, Mr. Salem," Jem replied.

"Carlos said you were upstairs using the table saw when Pete Zisk drove up. That's why you didn't hear anything?

115

"Yeah, we were finishing up the remodel then."

"Well, I had spoken to Homer the week before and he told me the inside was done. The only thing left was the front porch. When we got there, it was covered in fresh sawdust."

"Yeah," Jem said uneasily.

"I also noticed something had been dragged through that fresh sawdust recently."

Jem began to look around. He was obviously uncomfortable. "Were you really working upstairs, Jem?" Tom asked.

"Well, uh, I mean…," Jem stammered.

"You're a good kid, Jem. Lying doesn't come easily to you," Tom stated. "It's okay, tell me what really happened."

"I don't want to get in trouble, Mr. Salem," Jem pleaded.

"You won't. It's just us talking. I won't tell anyone else."

"We were working on the porch. The guy drives passed, and then a few minutes later he comes back. He drove up the drive and grandpa walked up to him. I didn't hear what they were saying the whole time, but grandpa obviously knew the guy. They started to argue and I heard grandpa tell 'em, 'I'm not gonna let you hurt him' and he drew his pistol. The guy pulled out the Taser and fired as grandpa was bringing up his gun. Grandpa started to shake and the gun went off, hitting the other guy. I ran to grandpa and kneeled down. He told me, 'I love ya, boy.' Then he coughed and said, 'tell Abel he's safe.' Then he was gone." Jem swallowed hard and continued, "I didn't want to tell the Sheriff what grandpa said about Abel, so I dragged the table saw upstairs and called them. When they got there, I told 'em I was upstairs." Jem breathed in deep.

Tom took a few seconds to process the information. "Did you tell Abel?"

"Yeah, we were at the house after grandpa's funeral. I told him what grandpa said and asked him what it meant. He told me the guy grandpa shot had threatened to hurt him, so grandpa was right. He was safe now."

"Thanks for telling me, Jem. I know it wasn't easy. Don't worry; your secret is safe with me."

They went back to their work. Tom could tell that Jem felt better after telling him the truth. They finished up their welding and parted for the day.

That night as Tom and Andrea watched TV together, Tom debated with himself whether or not to share this new information with Andrea. It was obvious that Abel could not live with the idea of people dying because of him. He planned his suicide for months, setting up the Will, getting life insurance, training Jem on all the little odds and ends of the farm and even cleaning his room. Tom had experienced a little of that himself.

Still, would his morality actually allow him to do it? After a while Tom realized that Abel likely didn't consider it suicide because he was making people safer by not being around them. He was saving people by dying. He probably had the missing pictures on his dash as he plunged the aircraft into the ground. Packing the cockpit with flammables as well as full tank of fuel ensured the heat of the fire would be enough to incinerate even his tough hide.

In the end, he decided it was better Andrea didn't know. She loved her brother more than anything and if she really believed he committed suicide it might be her mental undoing. She was tough, but even she had her breaking point. No, it was better for all that nobody ever knew the truth. He and Andrea would be married soon and all the sadness in the last few months would be pushed away. Was he selfish for not telling her? Maybe, but such is love.

Epilogue

One Year Later

Andrea made the climb down the side of the hill to Abel's former 'Exercise Yard.' She had come here alone once a month since his 'death' to read and pray. It was getting harder to get away alone with her being so far into her pregnancy, but Tom begrudgingly allowed her to make the trip by herself one last time. As usual, she had her large basket of sweet preserves and fresh bread.

She reached the tall wall of trees and sat on a soft, hollow log. She reached inside and pulled out an empty basket, replacing it with the new one. She then added a note that read:

Brother,

Some day you will have to be here so I can see you in person. I know you don't want me to see you, but I really would love to. Things are going well at the farm. My husband is becoming a regular Farmer John. Our hired man is as helpful as ever. Your niece or nephew will be coming soon and I don't think I will be able to come alone anymore. I'm not sure when I will be back, but I packed you some extra preserves this time. You must be getting tired of 'forest food' by now. I love and miss you more than I can say and hope that someday I will see you again.

Love,

Your Sister

Andrea was the only one that knew that Abel was still alive. Though he hadn't shown himself to her, the food was always taken and the empty basket left. Sure, it may have been someone else, but not likely. It was a relatively remote area with no trails and no nearby cabins.

Despite what she told Tom, she knew Abel could never commit suicide. It was a topic they had discussed many times and he was just too strongly against it. And he could easily have survived the crash. It would take extremely high temperatures for a long period of time to hurt him.

Andrea slowly climbed the side of the hill back to the old blue truck. She had one other appointment to keep. The realtor was meeting her to show her some nearby cabins that were for sale. She would use the life insurance money to buy one to use as a weekend vacation home for her growing family. It would allow her to be closer to Abel, too.

木木木

From across the river Abel stroked his newly-grown beard as he watched his sister amble up the hill and get in his truck. He missed that truck, but he missed her more. As she pulled away he thought about missing her pregnancy and was saddened. But things had to be this way. Once she was out of sight, he dropped down from the tree he had been sitting in and leapt over the river.

Abel walked up to the log and removed the items inside. He read the note and smiled. After placing the items in his backpack, he replaced the basket in the log. He then began the long trek home, jumping from tree to boulder to hillside, over and over until reaching his new home deep in the woods.

Abel had spent months building his tiny cabin in secrecy. There were no other cabins or trails within 20 miles. It was situated near a small stream under a rocky outcropping so it couldn't be seen even from the sky. Every Saturday his 'exercise' time had been spent falling trees and shaping rocks until he had built a sturdy one room log cabin. He had brought up a few solar panels and batteries that would provide lighting, and allow him to charge his tablet PC and run his tiny refrigerator. A small dresser contained some rugged clothing and his family pictures. His pantry was well-stocked with preserved food. He had a soft bed in the corner. All had been brought up in secret over a few months' time before he 'died.'

As he put away his new items, he thought about what brought him there. When Jem had told him what Homer had done, he decided right then he needed to get away. He could no longer justify what people had done for him to keep his secret. Homer had obviously known about his abilities, but never said anything. He had died to protect him and even more unfortunately, killed someone.

Abel thought of Andrea and how she came to him the night Rex 'left.' As he packed his clothes, Rex angrily told Andrea that, "Abel would be sorry for what he had done." Andrea, sick with the fear of losing her husband *and* her brother, had stabbed him in the back with a large kitchen knife. She came to Abel for help and he had buried the body in the garden and they told everyone Rex had run off. No one questioned it.

Luckily, he and Rex were about the same size and his remains made the perfect stand-in for him. It was not easy to dig up what was left of the body of his one-time best friend, but he did it and placed it in the aircraft along with some fire accelerants. After he crashed the plane, he made sure everything burned completely and thoroughly before leaving the scene.

121

Abel sat down on his bed and opened a jar of pickles. As he munched on them, he thought about his new life. He may have lost his family, but at least they were safer now. About once a week he hiked over near the small café in Ponderosa to use their Wi-Fi with his tablet to get caught up on the news of the day. He still got to help people occasionally and that was nice. There was even a small church in Springville he attended occasionally. It was a good life. Good enough, anyway.

The Healer – A Short Story

Larry Spence was sixteen years old when he finally accepted he was special. Sure, he and his parents had always known he was different. After all, he had never been sick a day in his short life. Even better, every cut or scrape he had ever had healed itself almost immediately. When he had fallen out of his tree house three years prior and snapped his arm, it had straightened and healed completely in less than a minute.

Larry knew his ability was a blessing for him and his parents. He hated to have to hide it, but understood from a young age that it was important to do so. But Larry's greatest desire was always to help other people. And at sixteen, he finally got his wish. And it all began with a simple mistake.

The family dog, Kai, had gotten out of the back yard early in the morning. She milled around the front of the house across the street until she saw Mr. Spence going to his car on his way to work. As he backed down the driveway, Kai was run over. The loud yelp of the injured dog made his dad stop the car and Larry and his mom came running from the house.

Kai lay under the car, gasping her last breath, blood oozing from her mouth and nose. Larry was the first to arrive and he pulled the dog from beneath the car and cradled the large Golden Retriever in his lap. He cried hard and hugged her tight.

The dog suddenly convulsed and began to breathe normally. She stood up and ran around the yard, frolicking happily. Larry's parents stared at him in amazement. His dad called the dog over and carefully inspected her for injury. The blood was still there, but had already dried. The dog had no apparent injuries.

The family of three spent the rest of the day together talking about what happened and examining the potential of Larry's gift. Mr. Spence, an amateur biologist, had found several dead insects and a dead bird. Larry tried to revive them all to no avail.

It was Mr. Spence that had the idea that maybe he could only revive injured or recently dead animals. He went to the local pet shop and bought a half-dozen white mice and brought them home. He held one under water for ten minutes. Convinced the animal was drowned, he handed the lifeless husk to Larry who concentrated hard on the animal. A few seconds later, the mouse coughed and gasped back to life.

Mr. Spence next used a razor blade to make a large cut on the back of another mouse. It was a grizzly thing to do, but he wanted to know exactly what his son was capable of. Larry cradled the bleeding mouse and a few seconds later, the wound was gone and only dried blood remained.

Mrs. Spence was convinced this new gift would be a curse. As a nurse, she explained to Larry that life and death are cycles, two sides of the same coin. It was hard enough for him to hide his own healing, but things lived and things died. As happy as they were that Kai was still with them, she should be dead, as Natural Law dictated. He should not 'play god' with people.

Mr. Spence disagreed. He considered this a 'gift from God' and was convinced Larry had been chosen by Him to do something special. It was hard to argue against his point with their beloved Kai still walking among them.

All were in agreement that this gift must be hidden like his other one. Larry was thankfully old enough to understand what the world would expect of him if they found out what he could do. There would be no healing others unless it could be kept secret and absolutely no bringing anything back to life.

***

Five years later, Larry was a pre-med student in his last year of college. He was volunteering as an EMT helper at a high school football game. The quarterback was hit hard and lay motionless on the field. Larry's supervisor, who had many years of experience, called for the backboard and they carefully strapped him to it. In the ambulance, the young man was awake but could not move his arms or legs. He was bleeding profusely from his mouth and ears. The more experienced EMT worked on him as Larry watched and handed him whatever equipment he needed. Several times, the EMT looked at Larry and shook his head solemnly. The boy wailed loudly.

As they neared the hospital, Larry took the quarterback's hand and squeezed it hard. He closed his eyes and concentrated. He knew he could save the boy's life and decided at that moment that it would be wrong of him not to do something when he had the ability to save him. The boy shuddered, then his arms and legs began to move wildly in their bindings.

As they unloaded him from the ambulance, the nurses took over. The EMT went inside with them as Larry and the driver began to clean up the ambulance. A few minutes later, the older EMT came out of the emergency room door, rubbing his head.

"I don't understand it," he explained. "That boy's spine was fractured, probably severed. I know it! His limbs were completely unresponsive to stimuli. His brain was bleeding. But he was just sitting up in his bed. He could move everything! Wasn't even in pain. I just don't get it." He shook his head as did the driver, another experienced EMT.

Larry was smiling and continued cleaning the ambulance and straightening things up. It was the first time he had broken the self-imposed rule, but he was pleased he had. He listened to the two men as they stood outside and talked for a few more minutes. Then they packed up and returned to the game.

***

One year later, Larry had graduated. While not at the top of his class, he did do very well. He had been accepted to several medical schools after scoring extremely high on his MCAT's. After speaking with an Army recruiter, it had been agreed that the government would pay for his medical school as long as he enlisted and served as an Army doctor for ten years afterward. At twenty-two years old, Larry was the happiest he had ever been.

Shortly after graduating, Larry and his family were driving home from morning church services. As they turned onto their block, their car was broadsided by a large truck. The world went dark for Larry, who had been sitting in the back seat.

When he awoke, he was laying on the road outside the mangled car. He felt fine and a quick run of his hands showed no damage to his body, but plenty of dried blood and torn clothing. He looked around feverishly for his parents. His father, who had been driving, was hanging out of the driver side door, his body twisted at an unnatural angle. He couldn't see his mom anywhere in the wreckage.

He quickly pulled his father from the car and checked his vitals, finding a weak pulse. Looking around to make sure no one was watching, he put both hands on his father's chest and concentrated. Seconds later his body was straightening out, cuts were closing and the color was returning to his face.

Mr. Spence opened his eyes and gasped. He sat up and hugged his son tightly.

"Your mother?" he asked frantically.

"I can't find her," Larry replied. They both knew that if she was in the wreckage and had died, Larry had only minutes to revive her before it was too late. And on top of that, people were pulling over and coming out of their homes to investigate and offer assistance.

They searched and searched, but the impact was on the passenger side, where his mother had been sitting. That side of the car was completely crumbled in on itself. They called out to her, but to no avail. Blood leaked from several cracks in the wreckage.

The fire department arrived and both men quickly tried to get them to use the 'jaws of life' to remove her, but seeing the wreckage, no one was in a hurry. Both had to be restrained by the police and EMT's, who assumed that given their bloodied and hysterical state, they must be suffering from injury. It was over an hour before the body of Mrs. Spence was extricated from the vehicle.

At the hospital, both men were found to be in perfect health. They were bloody, but neither had bruises or cuts. Mr. Spence had even lost the reoccurring pain in his arthritic right knee. He had never even thought to have Larry 'fix' it, but he had inadvertently done so that night. The doctors and nurses were confounded by the 'miracle.' The accident investigators were surprised, as well. If witnesses hadn't seen the other driver smash into them, they likely would have looked into the lack of injuries a little closer. They all assumed the blood must have belonged to the woman.

The driver of the other car was being worked on a few beds down from Larry and his dad. Larry stared at the team working hard to save the man's life. From the sound of things, they were fighting a losing battle. He heard a nurse stage whisper, "BAC 0.25" to the doctor, who looked over at him with a somber visage, then he quickly looked back at the patient.

Larry knew he could walk over to the bed and save the man's life with a single touch. His father had been in worse shape and he easily healed him. But it would mean exposing his gift to the world and he just couldn't do it. He wondered if he would do it if that was his mother. He decided he would.

Of course, the injured man had killed his mother. Even if he could easily revive him, Larry wasn't sure he would. He was in shock, still not accepting what had happened. He reminded himself, this man drank and drove and killed his mother. But he wanted him to face justice for what he had done!

Soon, it was apparent the medical crew had given up and called the time of death. Some began to move away while others started to clean up. Larry and his dad looked at each other, then began to walk over to the body. An orderly who was cleaning up the blood on the ground tried to intervene, but decided against it. The nurse who was cleaning the man up told them to move away, but Larry kept moving closer until he saw the man's face. Then he collapsed onto the dirty floor sobbing. The drunk driver who had killed his mom was the young quarterback he had saved the year prior.

It took many months for Larry to recover mentally. Mr. Spence stood by his son and never openly blamed him. Larry, however, blamed himself completely. The man would not have been alive to kill his mother had he not broke his own rule and saved him that night. With his father's help and the support of his church family, he finally began to forgive himself for what he had done. But never again would he "play god."

***

Six years had passed and Larry was an Army trauma surgeon stationed in Iraq. He had always requested duty in the most active parts of the war so he could do the most good. His father, always worried for his boy, spoke with him daily by phone or email.

While he had never broken his rule about saving a life outright with his gift, he had more than once ensured that soldiers would keep their limbs or recover from traumatic brain injuries. Their seemingly miraculous recoveries did not happen on the operating table but in their hospital beds afterward. He did not want any 'miracles' attributed to him.

Larry had honed his gift so well that he could heal one affliction without affecting another. That allowed him to heal an individual nerve or bone or muscle without healing the minor cut nearby. He could still heal an entire body, but never did as to better cover his tracks.

One evening, a female soldier was brought in who been caught in the blast of an Improvised Explosive Device. Her body had been broken and pierced in many places, but it was the major head wound that worried Larry the most. The explosive device had been wrapped in whatever junk the terrorists could find including some microscopic iron filings they secured from who knows where. The embedded iron filings were concentrated in her face and skull.

128

As the nurses worked on the soldier, he examined her head closely. Her face was shredded and would likely need extensive reconstruction for her to even be able to control her mouth or eyes. Even worse, the metal bits were scattered throughout her brain. She was alive and breathing, but he could never get it all cleaned out without destroying the tissue. He did his best and saved her life.

The next morning, Larry visited the soldier's bedside. She was comatose, as expected. Larry reviewed her chart and found she was doing surprisingly well, though her brain activity was almost nil.

Larry took a look around and gently grabbed the soldier's hand. He bowed his head and said a prayer. The field hospital personnel had seen him do it many times. After he finished praying, he concentrated hard and reached out into the soldier's body. He envisioned himself moving up the arm, though the shoulder and neck and into the brain. He 'saw' the damage and swelling and it began to subside. The tissues, torn and ragged, moved back together as if never apart. The tiny metal pieces became incorporated into the brain tissue as if it had never been separate.

Next, Larry moved through the eyes and into the underlying facial muscle and tendons. They began to knit together as well. He was able to complete most of the facial reconstruction before he was interrupted by a nurse yelling for him a few beds down.

"Doctor, he's crashing! We need you!" she yelled.

Larry took a quick glance at the solder, whose face was covered in bandages. "I'm on my way," he yelled back as he rose and put her hand back at her side. The soldier deserved a chance at a normal life. She deserved a family and babies and everything that goes with the American Dream. He had no idea what the metal in her brain would do, but he hoped that with a few more sessions, he could remove the metal completely and he could further reduce the scarring on her face.

Larry was kept busy the rest of his shift with other priorities and could not return to the soldier's bedside. The next morning, he came into the field hospital to do his rounds again. He was surprised to find the soldier's bed empty.

"What happened to the soldier that was in this bed?" he asked the duty nurse. "A girl, head trauma."

"Sargent Connelly? She was evac-ed this morning." The nurse handed him the soldier's chart, which she hadn't filed away yet.

"I didn't sign off on moving her!" he fumed.

"No, Dr. Peters did. He came in for his rounds at 2300 and found her vitals had improved substantially. I guess he wanted to get her someplace that could care for her better. Chopper left at 0600. I can find out where if you like."

Larry thought about it. "No, that's fine. Dr. Peters knows what he's doing. If he determined she was stable enough to travel, then I would agree." Larry did take note of the soldier's name and other personal information. He planned to look for her later, if possible. He was curious what would happen inside her head and if she needed further care, he would provide it. Off the record, of course. Given her many injuries, though, she would be out of this war, for sure. Maybe he would look her up stateside in a few years.

About the Author

Robert Whitbey grew up in Shafter, CA. He attended California State University, Bakersfield, the University of Wyoming and Point Loma University. He has been a high school science teacher for over a decade and an adjunct college professor for half that time. Prior to that he spent many years working in agricultural research. His hobbies include reading, writing, gardening and golf.

He has published a total of three books. His first, *How to Become a Reluctant Prepper and Why it's OK to be One*, was published in 2015 under his pen name, The Reluctant Prepper. His second book and first novel, *The Angel*, was published in 2016 and is a superhero fantasy novel based in California's Central Valley. It is first book of the Small Town Hero series. The second book in the series, *The Vessel*, was published in 2017 and takes place in Laramie, WY.

His favorite modern authors are Peter Clines, DJ Molle and Mark Tufo.

Rob currently resides in Bakersfield, CA with his wife, Lacy, and their two sons, Dylan and Jack.

The author asks for honest reviews when his books are finished.

You can get updates about the series by subscribing to our Facebook page at https://www.facebook.com/SmallTownHeroesSeries/